For Jeff who read the last page first …

Donna Lent

THE RISE OF GLOBAL: LABEL

Edited by Lorainne Kiley

A CIP catalogue record for this title is available from the British Library.

ISBN (Paperback) 9781739832964
ISBN (ebook) 9781739832933

First published in Swansea, Wales, United Kingdom, by Shelf Publishing.

THE RISE OF GLOBAL: LABEL is the second book in *THE RISE OF GLOBAL* trilogy.
THE RISE OF GLOBAL was previously published by Austin Macauley Publishers Ltd under the author name, Donna L. Jones.

Glossary

GS - Global Standard
MT - Mother Tongue
MLWA - Minority Languages World Association
GSPC - Global Standard Protocol Committee
GSW - Global Standard to the World
GSUA - Global Standard Unification Act
GSSW - Global Standard Saving the World (GSW's Charitable Organisation)

Prologue

As the sun endeavours to rise over Global Motherland and the Sub Motherlands, the "One Language, One Version, One Vision" label, which is the crowning glory of every skyscraper, illuminates more than the sun and moon, day and night. The red neon signs, which light up the skyline, fortify the status of Global Standard as the only permitted language.

Countries outside the Motherlands who have sworn allegiance to Global Standard to the World (GSW), to the Global Standard Protocol Committee (GSPC) and, have adopted Global Standard as their only language, adorn their tower blocks with the replicated adage.

Global Citizens are unified by their hearts and minds and believe wholeheartedly in the purpose and vision of Stephen Law and GSW. They are wholly invigorated by the colour they now associate with dawn. Not the natural glimmer of sunrise, but, the neon red which basks proudly in prominence and superiority. The RISE of Global Standard, as envisioned by Stephen Law, leader of the free Global world, has well and truly begun …

1

Relieved that her secondment had come to an end, Phoebe packed her belongings into a regulation GSW carrier bag. Trying to be the embodiment of Joan Marsh had been the hardest task of her life. When Phoebe received an unexpected email from GSW personnel, ordering her to return to her previous role, she had been thankful. Being secretary to Stephen Law, leader of the free Global world, affirmed to Phoebe that she did not, nor ever would, possess the same level of natural proficiency as Joan. Phoebe was certain her role had terminated because Joan was returning to her rightful place at GSW and at home.

Living in Joan's apartment illegally made Phoebe fearful that a random spot check would be carried out. Joan had left Global City so hastily that she hadn't taken Phoebe to the Foreigner's Office as they'd discussed, which meant that Phoebe was still an illegal – a fact, of course, unknown to Stephen Law. Phoebe's forged Global Citizen documentation had gained her employment at GSW and Joan's kindness had enabled her to leave the Straight Street squat to live in Joan's apartment in Global City.

However, Phoebe lived with continuous uncertainty that Mr. Law would uncover her Mother Tongue identity and unlawful status. The new Global Standard Language Law, which was being enforced throughout all GSW administered Global speaking countries, meant immediate eviction for illegals who, would not convert to Global Standard and consequently renounce their Mother Tongue. Joan's return was perfect timing and with Joan's assistance, Phoebe could, at last, become a legal Global Citizen.

Stephen Law had announced an amnesty whereby, all illegal citizens, if they swore allegiance to his Global Standard ideology of "One Language, One Version, One Vision" would be able to remain in Global City or any GSW region.

As Mr. Law's secretary, Phoebe had been privy to many edicts concerning Mother Tongue citizens on a global scale that made her extremely distressed and worried for her own safety and that of her family. Since the official launch of Global Standard many illegals, unwilling to renounce their Mother Tongue, had been forcibly removed from the Sub Motherlands and Global City. Phoebe was further disturbed because after exclusion, there was no paper trail or log of their whereabouts. Paradoxically, Phoebe had witnessed hundreds of illegals voluntarily presenting themselves to the GSPC who were overseeing their transition from Mother Tongue to official Global Citizens.

But, despite the amnesty, Phoebe did not have the courage to publicly declare that she had tricked Mr. Law. She knew that, despite her willingness to forsake her language, he would be furious that she had deceived him into employing an illegal to undertake one of the most trusted positions within GSW. It would be a humiliation he would struggle to handle. Phoebe believed that it would be better to wait for Joan to resolve the problem on her return. After all, Joan had uncovered Phoebe's illegal status before she left Global City and hadn't informed Mr. Law. As far as Phoebe was concerned, they were equally culpable.

Phoebe recalled how shocked Joan had been when she informed her that they both originate from the same region of Area Orange. How Phoebe had been sufficiently confident to leave home for a new life in Global City because of Joan's tenacity. Phoebe savoured telling her about the countless second-hand tales she had heard from her grandmother about how Joan was prospering since leaving their town. However, Phoebe shuddered when she recalled Joan's reprimand, "You have shunned your own family for life in Global City."

Joan's negative reaction had shocked Phoebe to the core and she suddenly felt very tense about seeing her again.

'Should I explain that the reason I followed her was out of admiration? Should I tell her about the many others from the Global Wave Generation who are ready to leave their homeland? A generation who genuinely believe that life in Global City is the only means to true happiness and prosperity. How they, too, want a share in the free Global world.'

Phoebe thought anxiously about her sister, Georgia and her friends and wondered why their venture was taking so long? Phoebe had paved the way; she had written to Georgia giving clear instructions how to make the journey. Phoebe had managed it, alone. What was taking her sister all this time? Phoebe felt tears seeping into the corners of her eyes. She was conscious that Mr. Law could be watching through the one-way glass which divided their office space. She wondered if he was pleased that Joan was returning. Phoebe composed herself and carried on packing, telling herself that she had to maintain her professionalism. There would be no pleasant exchanges just business as usual until she and Joan had the opportunity to see each other at home.

'Where is she?' Phoebe grumbled inwardly. 'The lift pinged ages ago. Maybe I should leave and pass her on my way out. Yes. That would be better. Then Mr. Law won't be able to observe,' she decided, opening her office door and entering the corridor. As she walked past the kitchen she stopped and watched a woman unpacking items from a cardboard box. Phoebe scrutinized the stranger as she neatly folded a Global Standard carrier bag and placed it in her handbag.

'This person looks like she's here to stay. Is it Joan?' Phoebe cogitated, looking at the back of the woman whose appearance looked vaguely familiar. Same size roughly, similar hair colour, same height and an identically immaculate appearance. Phoebe stood by the kitchen door and enquired timidly.

'Joan?'

The stranger turned around snappily, 'Joan. No. My name is Claudia and who are you?' 'Phoebe. I've been covering for Joan, um Miss Marsh while she's been … .' So that will make me the third Miss Marsh,' Claudia replied sarcastically.

Phoebe looked at her, confused, realising she had been replaced by this stranger and seemingly Joan wasn't returning to work after all. Her glib attitude made Phoebe question what she had done that was so wrong to be replaced by this person. Being Mr. Law's administrator was one of the most revered positions in Global City.

'Where is Miss Marsh? When my secondment was terminated I assumed Miss Marsh was returning to work.'

'Search me. I'm just following orders,' said Claudia, huffily.

'Your desk is through that doorway. Mr. Law's office is the other side of the glass. There's an adjoining door, but you never go into his office; certainly not uninvited. Not ever,' Phoebe emphasised. 'Would you like me to show you the way?' she enquired, contemplating whether she should forewarn Claudia about Mr. Law's minimalist employer-employee relationship.

‘No thank you. I’ll be fine,’ she quipped, marching assuredly away.

Phoebe stared after Claudia feeling quite incompetent, certain that, despite her apathetic attitude, Claudia would be a more capable, third Miss Marsh.

She doubted if she would ever see Joan again. Now, there were two people that she desperately needed and wanted to see who were missing from her life.

2

Georgia had no idea how much time had elapsed since she'd been captured by this distant shore. Was it minutes, hours, even days? She hazily recalled the rubber-dinghy style boat from which she and her friends had been thrown. She felt an overwhelming surge of remorse that they had decided to leave the safety of their hometown. She wondered at the naivety of their risk in believing they could navigate and accomplish this uncertain journey to Global City in a floating dirigible, little more durable than a plaything. The pounding waves pummelled her body, reminding her of the hostile, frantic sea that had lobbed her cruelly out of the dinghy. She drifted when the waves overwhelmed her and then sank into the seaweed and sand when they retreated.

'Where am I? Where are my friends?' she murmured, desperately, praying they had also washed up on shore alive. Amid the lashing of freezing, crashing water, her spirit urged, 'Now, get up, before the waves come back. Before your body smashes into the rocks again. Before your right ankle takes root once more between the jagged rock edges. Quick, now, you have at least ten seconds to move. Go on. You can do it. Move. Swiftly … too late, crash, smash, ride out the pain; try again in ten seconds. Count through the pain and it won't seem so bad. One, two, three … crash. Four, five, six … crash. Seven, eight, nine … crash. Ten … no pain. No feeling. No movement. Just nothing. All pain and feeling gone; crashed and smashed away.'

3

'I don't expect you to come back to Global City with me,' said Norman. 'I know you have rebuilt your life here since Dad died. But I must return to ensure that Mr. Law's plans for Global Standard are stopped. I owe it to Dad and to my great, great, great-grandfather. As the GSPC Director I'm still involved in any new legislation concerning Global Standard. I can't hide away any longer. I'm ready to do whatever is necessary to protect our language in this region of Motherland and all Mother Tongues who do not want to be subjected to Global Standard.'

'But you are my life,' she responded. 'Wherever you go, I go.'

'Once we are back in Global City, you may not like my plan. It will mean acting out of character for us both.'

'Oh!' she replied. 'I'm intrigued.'

'I was going to resign,' Norman began. 'The last time Dad came to my office, the day he died; I had my resignation letter ready for David. Despite our friendship, David's the boss, so I thought I should make it official. The note explained that because of Dad's dementia degenerating I needed to be at home. You needed me, Dad needed me,' said Norman, tearfully. 'Then Dad … then Dad … ,' he paused, finding it difficult to continue, remembering painfully how his father had passed away, without warning.

'I can still smell the newspaper he was holding; the broadsheet that he insisted on reading every day. Remember how he'd hold it upright and all you'd be able to see of him was his crossed legs, relaxing. I often wondered how he could sit motionless, for so long. He wouldn't turn the pages, he'd just open it and whatever page he happened on, that would be the page he'd read, over and over. I was so distracted that day, composing and re-writing my resignation letter.

'Then I said, "Ready Dad?" because usually that would be the trigger to pull him out of his reverie. But that day, that awful, awful day, I said, "Ready Dad? Dad, are you ready?" When he didn't respond, I didn't think anything at first but after my third request and he still hadn't answered, I had this feeling of foreboding, which I thought was some silly, irrational emotion. But … well, you know the rest. He'd gone, just like that, in complete silence. Gone.'

Linda was relieved that Norman was at last talking about that day. He needed to chat about it; he needed to let go of his grief. She knew him well and festering was not a good thing.

'Dad's dementia was only half the truth,' he continued, unburdening. 'The full version is that I was ashamed that I could be involved with Stephen Law after all those years of hearing Dad's "old, old story" about how my great, great, great-grandfather fought to uphold our ancestral language. How could I continue working for the GSPC knowing they support Stephen's plan to eradicate all vernaculars? His plan to spearhead Global Standard as the one common language of the world? How could I stand back and watch them use our homeland as the "guinea pig blueprint"? I realised that I couldn't turn a blind eye to the tyranny that Mr. Law is planning to exact on those who refuse to renounce their Mother Tongue in favour of Global Standard.'

'I had no idea you felt this way Norman,' murmured Linda, surprised. 'Why didn't you tell me you were conflicted working for the GSPC?'

‘Because money talks,’ he replied, ashamedly. ‘The five-year contract as the GSPC Director, which included the Profit Share for Life Scheme, seemed too good to be true.’

‘Five years, I thought. Five years is no time at all. I had it all planned. The salary itself is more than most people earn in a lifetime. Five years and we would be set financially for the rest of our lives. Then I would retire and we could return home, here, for good. I wanted so badly for us to leave Global City, to take Dad home; to surround ourselves with our friends once more, in this wonderful town. I’m convinced Dad would have been cured of dementia by being with the people and things which were known to him; I honestly believe this familiarity would have made him better. He wouldn’t have had to strain his faculties to speak a language that he learned, yet never fully embraced. It was just a means to an end for him. It was our fault. We brought Global into his life. We should have stayed with him at home. We should have realised that uprooting an ageing man and expecting him to adapt to city life, would have repercussions. We as good as killed him.’

‘Norman, this is your grief talking. We loved him. We looked after him. He was happy. He adored living in the city. He was an intelligent man who recognised that we had given him a new adventure in later life. It was the illness that killed him, Norman. You must accept that or you’ll become ill yourself. In between his lapses, he knew his own mind. You’ve just said that he was able to recite the old, old story. He remembered how his great, great-grandfather had gumption; just like his own determined spirit.’

‘But that’s precisely the point, Linda. Don’t you see? Why else would he have repeated that same story? It was his way of telling us that he didn't belong in Global City; that WE don't belong there. It was his way of reminding us of our heritage, our culture and language. It was his way of expressing that deep down, in his spirit, he wanted to return home. Back to the place where it all began; to the place where his character was formed. To the place where his memories and friends were, people of his own generation with whom he shared so much. He should have died at home, not in that awful, lonely city that sucks you in and spits you out, where the people are so full of avarice. People, just like Stephen Law who live for status and opportunity. Even as Dad lay dead in my office, he used my grief for his own agenda. Even the paramedic believed that Dad was Stephen Law's grandfather.'

'What do you mean? You never told me he was there that day. You said the paramedics came … ,' said Linda, confused. 'And why did the paramedic assume that Dad was Stephen's grandfather? I know the age difference would have made it a possibility, but to make such an assumption, I don't understand.'

'Stephen came before the paramedics,' snorted Norman angrily. 'He barged in, trying to lay down his rule of law. He told me that he had sent Rod Jones to Area Blue to take care of my failure and that Rod would succeed where I had not. That must have been a lie because even though we don't venture into town much, I'm sure over the last few months we would have bumped into Rod at some point. Plus, I think we would have noticed if the right to speak our Mother Tongue had been halted.'

'But still, why did the paramedic think that Dad was Mr. Law's relative?' asked Linda, agitatedly.

Norman looked intently at Linda, 'Because I don't believe Stephen Law originates from Global City; despite him being the epitome of Global. I believe he has a secret ethnicity and Global isn't his birth language.'

'What?' said Linda, alarmed.

'That day, when he saw Dad lying on the settee, he cried out in distress, as if it were him who was bereaved. But, instead of calling out in Global Standard, he used a foreign language. His cry of anguish didn't sink in at first. Like you, I assumed the paramedic thought they were related because of the generation gap which would have been a plausible error. But after replaying every moment of that day over and over in my mind, I kept coming back to one word. To that one moment when Stephen turned around, saw Dad and blurted out in despair. He not only cried out but did so in a language that the paramedic understood. That's why he assumed Dad was his grandfather. The word that Stephen used when translated into Global Standard means exactly that, grandfather. It took me quite a while to recall the word. I wrote it down in so many ways because I didn't know how to accurately spell it. Then, I input the word into the Global Translate Technology device which converts a Mother Tongue word instantly into Global Standard and vice versa, and, lo and behold, the word means grandfather in the Mother Tongue of the other country that Stephen labelled orange on the GSW world map. Why he wanted two areas coded orange I still don't know. Why he never reprimanded me for colour coding our hometown blue when he was insistent he wanted it to be orange is of an equal mystery.'

'So what are you saying Norman? Are you implying that Stephen Law is not a Global thoroughbred? He doesn't originate from Motherland?

'Yes, that's exactly what I'm saying. The Global Standard form affords the word no justice at all. This is the beauty of Mother Tongues. The meaning of words goes so much deeper than Global Standard implies. The meaning of grandfather in the language Stephen spoke that day is "ancestral person to whom one goes for wisdom". The paramedic who, without doubt, was an illegal citizen tried to deny any understanding of the word by saying that he thought Stephen was the grandson because of his distressed tone. It's ironic that the paramedic did not realise that he had witnessed the leader of the free Global world speaking in a Mother Tongue!'

'How did you have one of those GSW devices? You told me that he is keeping them covert?' asked Linda, further bewildered.

'That's not important. The point is Stephen Law is a fraud! He's the most significant illegal citizen in Global City. To have knowledge of the word that he uttered, he must originate from Area Orange,' said Norman, pointing on his map.

'I, we, will ensure that his outrageous plans are stopped and his identity revealed.'

'But how are we going to do that? How many times have you told me that he is ruthless when it comes to Global Standard? How are we going to stop someone like him? What about David? Does he know any of this? Don't you think you should tell him?'

'David lives his life based on profit margin alone. He has no sentimentality when it comes to family, culture or history. One common, simplified, standardised language would suit him perfectly.'

'But I still don't understand what we can do to stop their plans, especially if David believes there will be a lot of money to be made.'

'Just have faith, Linda. Where there's a will, there's a way,' retorted Norman, optimistically.

4

Rod missed his sister, Angelina. This was not part of his remit. Being separated from her was not his intent when he arranged for her to join him in Global City. When Mr. Law ordered him to Mother Tongue Area Blue to secure the Global Standard situation that Norman had failed to accomplish, Rod thought it would be a quick fix. Rod hadn't been in contact with Angelina since arriving at Area Blue. Mr. Law had forbidden it. Before Rod left Global City, Stephen gave him explicit instructions to ensure he carried out his duties as his Language Warrior and The Face of GSW without interference. He did not want Rod distracted by anything or anyone and that included Angelina. Rod had no idea that this communication embargo would keep him covert for such a long time.

Also, before he left, Rod was under the impression that Mr. Law had prepared the way prior to his arrival. He believed himself to be merely the errand boy sent to collect the signed Global Standard Language Treaty (which was endorsed by the GSPC, despite Norman's absence) from the Education Minister and return it to Global City immediately. Mr. Law had, so Rod thought, taken care of all the details and arranged all the necessary meetings prior to Rod's arrival. But, the Education Minister hadn't signed the Treaty for Global Standard to oust Area Blue's ancestral Mother Tongue. Rod was surprised at how patient Mr. Law was with the Minister.

As Rod sat in his hotel room, looking at the view that had become his temporary home, he felt nostalgic; not for Global City, but his own homeland, the place where his parents lived. He thought despairingly about the Global

City skyscrapers with the artificial neon red that beamed "One Language, One Version, One Vision" around the city. He marvelled at Area Blue's natural light; revelling in the peace and tranquillity it generated. He didn't sleep well in Global City because the permanency of the neon lights always interrupted his rest. Blackout curtains were forbidden in all Global Standard speaking countries. This ensured the Global Standard mantra shone as brightly as the sun, day, and night.

Rod was missing Angelina, but, conversely, he was also enjoying the freedom of this region of Global Motherland. The longer he stayed in Area Blue, the more he longed to hear his own language once more. The more he wanted to speak in his Mother Tongue again. But Mr. Law had forbidden him to have contact with anyone other than the Education Minister and his five staff. These five people had assured Rod, in Global Standard, at various times that the Education Minister would be signing the necessary documents imminently.

Stephen may have taken away Rod's liberty to communicate with residents of Area Blue and his sister, but he had not prohibited him from exploring the area. It was on these occasions that Rod's yearning for his own culture and language started to become poignant. As he drove past schools he heard the Mother Tongue babble of children, happy and singing as they played. Outside churches he heard bells ring with exuberance. Even the chimes seemed to echo this region's ancestral language. As he walked and listened to the older generation chatting away, those his parents age, he felt in awe of their contentment. As he witnessed the celebration of their "Language Day", when children and adults alike adorned their national dress, he felt anger towards his mother for propelling him on a path for which he had no longing; all in the name of status and opportunity.

Area Blue reminded him in so many ways of his own homeland, but there were differences. This region seemed to have an air of satisfaction which oozed from the youngest to the oldest. Rod felt like a charlatan as he sat and witnessed the lives of these people who had no idea that their language and way of life was about to be eradicated.

'Why?' he asked himself despairingly, 'why did I allow my mother to convince me that I needed to leave home to prosper? Why am I allowing Mr. Law to manipulate me?' As Rod continued to observe Area Blue citizens, he pondered how he could resign his position. He did not want to be the face of GSW. He longed to look at his reflection in the mirror and recognise his face; recognise the person he used to be before Global City. He needed to be Nimrod Nazareth again. But he had no idea how to stop Mr. Law marching into Area Blue and claiming it as a Global Standard region.

5

'Help me, please,' whimpered Georgia despairingly in her Mother Tongue.

'Please … ,' her voice tapered.

A group of young children peered from a distance with a mixture of curiosity and distress as they heard Georgia's pitiful cries. They could not comprehend what she was saying as they didn't understand her native tongue. But the desperation in her voice caused one child's inquisitiveness to follow the noise to where her body lay. The other children trailed behind but stopped suddenly as their friend dropped her bucket and spade, turned, ran straight passed them, shrieking as she went. The children that were left, edged closer to Georgia's broken body that was oozing blood and puss, just like one of the squashed worms in their buckets. Another child screamed and ran frantically back to the safety of her parents. The remainder followed suit, also screeching alarmingly as they ran.

Norman and Linda sat in their beach hut, admiring the view and pondering their return to Global City. When Norman's father died and Norman told Linda he needed to leave Global City for a while, she had no idea that he intended to return to their seaside town. Yet she should have realised that home would be the only place where Norman and she, for that matter, would find solace. Before Norman's Dad had moved to Global City their home and beach hut had been a retreat. A sanctuary to where they returned when the city began to take its toll. Norman was so glad he had kept his family home by the sea where he grew up. Despite Stephen Law's command that this region of Motherland should be colour coded orange, Norman had coded it blue because of his fond memories of the aqua blue sea

Norman felt great pleasure that, not only had he defied Mr. Law's order, but that he still had no inkling that Area Blue was his ancestral home. Oh the comfort Norman felt when his friends spoke fondly about his late parents! Initially, Norman's father coped well when his wife had died. He refused to be a burden to Norman and Linda and remained in the family home, insisting he was more than able to take care of himself. He had been adamant that the two of them should continue with their own lives in Global City. But all that changed quite suddenly when a frantic phone call from his dear friend, Jim, transformed Norman and Linda's lives completely.

"He's okay, Norman, but he gave me such a scare. I don't know what came over him, thinking he could go swimming that time of night. It was a good job I hadn't caught my usual hoard of snapper fish the day before. That's the only thing that sent me back out to sea, it being my day off and all. You can't imagine the fright I had seeing him washed up on shore. I thought he was dead. I was pumping his chest thinking that however much water he'd swallowed needed to spurt out and quickly. I nearly gave up. My knees had sunk so deeply into the sand and the tide was coming in. The light from the boat was bouncing up and down with the waves making it nearly impossible to see. Then, with one last push down on his chest out came the water, like the sea creature ejected Jonah. He's had a chest x-ray and his lungs are clear but he is very confused, Norman. You really need to come home."

Norman sat looking out to sea, remembering how Jim had saved his father's life. He was thankful that, despite the unexpectedness of his dad's death that day in his office, at least Norman had been with him. At the very minimum, his father knew he was loved.

'Look at those little ones,' said Linda, interrupting his trance as she pointed to the children who were sprinting as fast as they could in the direction of their parents and screaming at the tops of their voices.

As they got closer to Norman and Linda it was evident from the troubled look on their faces and the pitch of their wails, that screaming wasn't part of their game.

Distressing memories of his father's near drowning gripped Norman causing him to leap out of his deckchair and run in a contra flow to the children. As he made his way across the beach he saw a few brightly coloured objects scattered haphazardly in the distance. He continued to run in the direction of the items, realising that they were the children's deserted buckets and spades. As he got closer to the shoreline, one final bucket and spade lay discarded. The worms and shells that had been dug up were abandoned in a heap. As Norman stood at the shoreline, wondering what the children had been running from, he saw a bright orange lifejacket flung casually over some rocks at the entrance to the cove. Jim's words reverberated in his mind as he pictured his lifeless father, half drowned and all alone. Norman had seen lifejackets from the boats washed up on shore before but something felt amiss about this one. The children were evidently fleeing scared. Norman looked back to the children who were taking comfort from their parents. In the distance he saw Linda powerwalking towards him, waving her hands frantically. He picked up the life jacket and inspected the area until his eyes fell upon a skewered body. Norman motioned frantically at Linda to hurry up.

A numbing pain engulfed Georgia's whole being. During bouts of consciousness she realised she was alive due to the frantic pulsating in her head which was mirrored by her heartbeat. Underneath her sodden clothing her wounded torso yearned for her homeland, for her own bed, for her mother's embrace. It was not meant to be this way.

She was supposed to be safe and prospering in Global City along with her sister and with her friends from her town who'd also left. Georgia had no idea that the Global language she'd been secretly learning to enter the free Global world had been superseded by Global Standard. She had no notion that the stakes for access into Global City had escalated out of her reach. She did not know she had washed ashore in a land where there was as strong a resistance to Global as in her own country.

Norman looked down in disbelief at this young woman's broken body. Her hair was braided with seaweed and sand. He bent to lift her head out of the water, wondering if she was dead or alive. He put his hands underneath her back and attempted to lift her. As he did, the nameless young woman winced in pain, affirming that she was indeed alive. Norman could see that her ankle was caught between two jagged rock edges. He dug his hands deep into the sand to try to liberate her. Linda gasped in shock at the sight of the castaway that had somehow washed up on their shore.

'Hold her head up,' instructed Norman, as he attempted to free her ankle. 'I dread to think how much sea water she's already swallowed.'

Tenderly, Linda nestled her head and removed the green algae from her face. Her nostrils were encrusted with sand as were her nails as they had dug into the grit trying to find pain relief.

Linda was horrified to see that the castaway was just a young girl, a young girl who belonged to somebody;

whose family were probably at their wits end, worrying about her whereabouts.

6

Phoebe opened her office draw and gazed at Joan's inactive mini pc, Global Citizen Identity Card and Global Citizen Passport that were in her safe keeping.

'If Joan has boarded a plane she must have done so as a Mother Tongue citizen,' she thought; a secret identity of whom only she and Phoebe knew. Phoebe pondered if there was any significance to this. Mr. Law had no idea that Joan, like herself, was of Mother Tongue heritage. Phoebe was puzzled why Joan had decided not to take her Global identity with her.

When Phoebe had been discharged from her role as Mr. Law's administrator and decided that Joan's belongings should leave with her, it had been a bold move. For the whole time she had been Joan Marsh, Phoebe had not alerted Mr. Law to Joan's abandonment of the items. Firstly, because Phoebe did not have that type of relationship with him and secondly, she realised that he might take it as a sign of Joan's disloyalty or, worse still, she did not plan to resume her job. As time passed and Joan had not returned, Phoebe struggled with the urge to switch on the device. However, she resisted the temptation as she'd been too anxious to do it. She thought that as soon as she switched it on, Mr. Law would be alerted to its activity. He may even think that it was Joan herself reactivating it, she deduced, woefully. So, it would be her secret possession, but it would stay turned off. It would remain inactive until Joan herself switched it back on.

7

Joan's happiness beamed from within as her new mother-in-law, Dorcas, proudly pushed a wedding surprise through a jubilant crowd of guests. Excited gasps could be heard in anticipation of what was hidden underneath the gold, hand-embroidered, satin cloth. Joan had no inkling what was concealed beneath the loosely draped material. As she stood, immersed in love, Joan suddenly realised this was the only wedding she had ever attended and here she was, not just a guest, but the bride. Her own wedding day was her introduction to one of her town's most revered celebrations. Despite Joan being the first daughter to marry within her family, her parents and sisters seemed extremely familiar with the proceedings. Joan felt saddened as she realised that for all the years she had lived in Global City, she had missed numerous weddings and festivities. While she had been away, her family participated, without her.

As the gasps continued and enthusiastic applause began, Joan sensed that she was the only one who did not actually know what the mysterious object was. Joan wondered if this display of oneness was a wedding tradition that expressed town life. She felt overwhelmed by the sense of togetherness that surrounded her. For a slight moment she felt like a stranger; like she didn't belong with these people, unworthy to be amongst folk who had no idea that she had two identities. Joan panicked inwardly and didn't know whether she could continue with the charade. But she had already exchanged vows; she'd already had the opportunity to protest her own deception.

The groom gazed at his radiant bride almost in disbelief that she had accepted his marriage proposal. After all, they had only been together a short time. But he felt as if he'd known Aphia, as she was called, all his life. Joan looked at her husband, overwhelmed by his love for her which was etched across his face, wondering when she should tell him the truth. Tell him, that, 'Yes, I am Aphia Joan from our hometown; yes, my family are now your family and will love you like a son and brother, but I didn't look after my elderly grandmother in the mountain village as I told you when we first met. That was a lie; that was to protect myself and my family. The truth is … the truth is, for the last four years I have lived in Global City as secretary to the leader of the free Global world.

This man, Stephen Law, wants to wreak havoc in countries like ours. He wants to obliterate our vernacular and way of life. Ashamedly, I played a huge part in the launch of Global Standard; a version of Global that is now an official language in Global Motherland and beyond. A language philosophy that has the backing of the GSPC, who, along with Mr. Law, are convincing other country leaders that Global Standard, is the way forward. That adopting Global Standard as their country's official tongue will ensure its citizens are not left behind in this "Global Wave" of language superiority. My name for the past four years has been Joan Marsh, Global Citizen number …,' she finished, exasperated by her own truth. Joan looked at her wedding guests, realising it wasn't just her husband she was deceiving but the whole town. Her lie had led him to believe that she had been living in the mountain village all these years … .

"I'm confounded that you have been so near to me, even possibly when we were younger, yet I never knew you. But that's all changed because now I plan to never let you out of my sight," he'd lovingly told her, the day he proposed. He thought their life was perfect. He was prospering as Mayor, plus, he was upholding his promise to his predecessor, Jakov, who held that office for forty years, to ensure that Global was kept out of their country, town and lives, no matter what the cost.

In fact, Grigor's candour to honour Jakov's dedication to Mother Tongue had been emulated by each of the districts in his homeland. This gave Grigor the extra peace of mind he sought concerning Global. His people, indeed, the nation's people, rejected it. They did not need to communicate in it to succeed. Global speaking tourists did generate much needed revenue, even Jakov acknowledged that. But, if the consequences of Grigor's NO GLOBAL remit meant losing all Global speaking tourists, so be it. Jakov's vision for their country was still his priority and he would never allow anyone to compromise his promise.

'Aphia,' called Dorcas affectionately. Joan was still getting used to being called by her childhood name. For the past four years her Global Citizen nomenclature was Joan Marsh. How wonderful it was to be called Aphia once more. Her parents and sisters did not know her as Joan, so for them it seemed natural. As soon as she arrived home, her family addressed her as Aphia. Joan Marsh was not a person with whom they were acquainted.

'Grigor, you too. Come,' his mother motioned excitedly.

Hand in hand, Aphia and Grigor walked over to the hostess trolley. Grigor, like the other guests, knew what was underneath the cloth. Aphia, unsure if this was customary or unique to her wedding, began to exude an enigmatic smile, a mixture of happiness and nerves.

The lights in the hall were extinguished as Dorcas expertly whisked off the cloth and within seconds lit a multitude of candles that started sizzling away. Each tier had different coloured sparkles which enabled the bride, groom and wedding guests to see Dorcas' masterpiece. The guests began to applaud the ziggurat style wedding cake. Each layer of moist sponge had a colour that matched its flavour; orange for mandarin, red for strawberry, yellow for lemon, cream for vanilla and russet for chocolate. The top tier of all was decorated with white icing. Dorcas handmade sugar poppies in their different seasonal colours of red, orange, yellow, purple and blue around the rim. In pride of place on the top sat tiny, delicately crafted, polymer bride and groom figures that looked as if they were about to blossom into life. Dorcas picked up the serrated knife and handed it to Aphia. As the candles fizzled and the flash from the photographer took over, Grigor lovingly placed his hand over Aphia's. In one motion, they sliced down into the cake, offering the first piece to a very worthy recipient.

'Thank you,' beamed Dorcas proudly in their Mother Tongue as the guests waited for her to take a bite and declare it "good to eat", as was their tradition.

'It's very tasty, even though I am biased!' she blurted out laughing with joy as the guests cheered once more.

As Aphia and Grigor cut slice after slice of wedding cake, Aphia thought she saw Stephen standing at the back of the room.

'Are you okay?' Grigor asked, noticing that her hand had become clammy.

'Yes, I've never been better,' she smiled, aware that her mind was playing tricks. She realised that the last time she had seen Stephen, he, too, had been cutting into a similar style cake at the Global Standard launch party.

Aphia looked around at her family and the assembled guests she had known since childhood. How she loved the chatter of her Mother Tongue. The very sound of their language gave her a true sense of identity. It filled her heart with so many wonderful memories of growing up in this close-knit community. Her anxiety that she would utter Global responses instead of speaking in Mother Tongue had long gone. As each day passed at home, her own language seeped through her very soul. In fact, each day gone that she hadn't communicated in Global, further removed her from the events of the past four years in Global City. Aphia looked once more at the spot where she thought she had seen Stephen and, to her relief, he was not there. The thought of him gave her a cold shudder.

Fleetingly, she wondered who was sitting at her desk in her absence. It reminded her that she somehow had to contact Phoebe to tell her she wasn't returning to Global City. She didn't know what she would tell her, the truth or a lie? Aphia didn't know if she trusted Phoebe enough to keep her location a secret from Mr. Law. Not because Phoebe was dishonest but because Mr. Law had a way of extricating information from unwitting people. Telling Phoebe would make her vulnerable. Sharing a lie could be oppressive. Aphia felt sickened by the deceit she was keeping from Grigor. She felt full of shame and burdened that the lie had only just begun and it was up to her to stop it; except, she didn't know how.

As Grigor watched his parents chatting with guests and looking so happy, his mother's traditional approval of the cake transported him back to his childhood. Year after year, birthday after birthday, she had steadfastly baked the same style for their family and closest friends, Apollos and Nastan Popov. He recalled fondly how Apollos had always commented that the ziggurat shape reminded him of the description of the Tower of Babel from the Bible. He remembered how he would sit with Apollos for hours discussing how they, along with Jakov, would ensure their Mother Tongue was upheld within their town and country. How they would ensure that Global would never replace their beloved language. He recollected how Nastan would joke that Grigor should have been born into his family because he was more like a grandson to Apollos than he. He jested that Grigor had more in common with his grandfather.

'Nastan Popov,' thought Grigor in his usual guarded manner, wondering where in the world he was, pondering if he was still obsessed with Global. He puzzled why, today of all days, his thoughts of Nastan were stronger than usual.

Grigor dismissed him to a dark recess of his mind, unaware that Nastan, as he once knew him, no longer existed. Stephen Law had usurped him many years ago. And the reason old thoughts had arisen concerning Nastan Popov were much closer to home than he could possibly imagine.

8

Stephen looked in the mirror, overall pleased with the grey streaks in his hair. He glanced at his father's photograph that was tucked into the mirror's frame and smiled at how alike they were. He studied the faceless mannequin that stood expressionless in the corner of his living room sporting a Language Monitor uniform, satisfied with the finished product. The blueprint for the uniform's design formed a blanket on his bed, along with the draft for the Global Standard to the World flag.

He looked poignantly at the plans and recalled, vividly, his first night at the International School where he'd spent his teenage years. He remembered his excitement as he'd discovered his father's ideas for replacing his Mother Tongue with Global.

He gathered the papers and placed them in his briefcase; the same one that his father had used to store his Global research. The briefcase still contained Stephen's late father's original Global papers, maps, diagrams and speech. The speech that his father never had the opportunity to present at the International Translator's Conference. The monastery bombing which killed his father, his mother, Lydia and grandmother, Damaris.

The speech that, as Global Language Ambassador for his country, would have ushered in a new Global Wave. Over three decades later, the very same briefcase, now battered and wrinkled with wear, contained, not only Stephen's father's papers, but a host of fresh ideas composed by a man who believed that the Global phenomenon he had orchestrated was in the way of tribute to his papa. But sadly, the only thing that the two men had in common was a name. All Stephen's other traits were being manipulated by his disjointed sense of grief and the Invisible Stranger, whom he had warily grown to trust, like a father figure … .

9

For a few minutes before Georgia fully awoke, she forgot about the time-consuming arduous journey she had made to follow her sister to Global City. For a split second, as her head snuggled into the pillow and her body was wrapped warmly in the quilt that cocooned her, in those semi-conscious waking moments, she was home. She was safe. Her mother, father and Phoebe were downstairs making breakfast and in an instant her mother would call, saying that it was time to get up. It was time to start a brand-new day. It was time ... .

'How did you sleep?' enquired Linda gently, bringing Georgia back to reality.

'Very well, thank you,' answered Georgia in her Mother Tongue, before correcting herself to respond in Global.

'Your face is healing nicely,' said Linda positively.
'Yes, I feel much better,' murmured Georgia.

'You are a sight for sore eyes,' uttered Norman chirpily, entering the room.

Have you remembered how you ended up on our shore, like a mermaid,' asked Norman tenderly in Global. Georgia felt flustered. She recalled vividly how she had washed up on this foreign beach. She knew only too well the deceit and betrayal that had sealed her fate. But she wasn't ready to tell the tale just yet, so pretending that she couldn't remember was the safest option.

10

'Where are we going so early in the morning?' asked a tired Aphia.

'I'm taking you home,' replied Grigor.

'Home?' thought Aphia, deeply concerned what Grigor meant by home.

'I shouldn't have been so thoughtless,' he continued, packing an overnight bag. 'I should have realised that you would be missing your old life. I'm sorry. I've been so busy planning the Language Town that I have neglected to consider your feelings.'

Aphia looked at him in trepidation. The butterflies in her stomach were fluttering with worry. 'Has someone discovered the truth about me? Has someone betrayed me?' she wondered; panic stricken.

'There's no need to pretend any longer Aphia. I know how you have pined for your old way of life. Your sister, Noadiah, spoke to me. She told me how you are desperate to go home. How you long to breathe in the mountain air, to wake and see the sunrise sitting on the mountain peak, just as you used to, during all those years caring for your grandmother.'

'Noadiah knows me too well it would seem,' said Aphia, with forced laughter playing along with her sister's trickery. She didn't know why her little sister would have said all these untruths to Grigor but she knew that, for the sake of her family, she had to acquiesce.

'Home?' Aphia repeated questioningly.

'To the mountain village. Where else? I suppose it's still your home after spending so many years there.'

'But here is home, Grigor. The mountain was somewhere I lived out of necessity. I can assure you that the mountain is truly out of my system. You, the town and our families are home to me these days.'

Oblivious to Aphia's reluctance, Grigor said, 'I'll collect wood for the stove. I'm really looking forward to the peace and tranquillity. We deserve a break; we haven't had a honeymoon. It's great that your family held onto your grandmother's house. It can be our weekend retreat.'

Aphia watched him walk away. He seemed so happy. Aphia had been dreading this day. She had feared the time when her lies would begin to envelop her. However, she hadn't expected that day would be so soon or would come by way of her baby sister.

11

Stephen stood on his balcony, stretched out his arms and whistled the familiar early morning call to his loyal mourning doves. They instantly perched on his hands, eating their usual seed. He stood statue-like, basking in the true colour of dawn; the neon red that all Global Citizens associate with the start of a new day. The luminous scarlet glare from the "One Language, One Version, One Vision" signs reflected on his face, heating his complexion like the furnaces in the GSW dungeon that destroy all illicit Mother Tongue literature, in all formats, day and night.

Stephen watched contentedly as the mourning doves fluttered back to their young. He stood facing his mirror and began to rehearse his speech once more …

'Ladies and Gentlemen of the Global Standard community; I am Stephen Law the founder and CEO of Global Standard to the World. I am truly honoured to have been invited to this hallowed building today which has hosted some of the world's greatest visionaries. I am humbled to share with you my vision for taking Global Standard to the ends of the earth.

'But firstly, I would like to pay homage to the person who gave me the vision for this crusade; a man who, sadly, is only here in spirit; a man who wasn't afraid to go after what he believed and had the original idea for Global replacing all Mother Tongues – my late father. Thanks to his inspirational forward thinking, the potential for Global Standard to the world is limitless as we embark on this wonderful language adventure. The vision of Global Standard is to unite all people, all nations and all cultures into one holistic family. But how will we do this?

‘We will do this by equipping all schools, even the smallest in the most remote areas with a hand-held, mobile device that translates their Mother Tongue into Global Standard. No longer will there be a divide between those who can communicate and those who cannot. The hiatus between rich and poor will be banished. People from every language and culture will be given the opportunity to learn and speak Global Standard – a true language gift from me to the world. GSW and the GSPC believe that making Global Standard uniform will enable Mother Tongue citizens everywhere to interact with each other in confidence. Consider the benefits of one common vernacular; no communication barriers, no expensive interpretation costs, no limitations to trade or medicine. Global Standard’s Translate Technology will enable citizens across the planet to decode their Mother Tongue with ease, while simultaneously enabling them to learn Global Standard. Standardising Global will allow all people to access the language in one version that they will, eventually understand. There won’t be any alien accents, dialects or phrases to contend with; just one, pure Global Standard form, which will be easily understood and spoken by all.

‘GSW and the GSPC have already made available a new Global Standard Dictionary which was given out to Motherland and Sub Motherland citizens on Global Standard launch day. This dictionary has become the most sought-after book of words in the modern era. We have ensured that it’s available free of charge to all Global Citizens. If you haven’t already acquired a copy, then please feel free to collect one on your way out.

‘But what about the costs for access to such technology? There will be a nominal licence fee for each unit which will devolve to the purchasing countries. GSW and the GSPC do not exist for profit but for the greater good. Speaking of which, this gadget has the power to save lives. Indeed, this gadget has already saved a life and will enable this to happen more and more. Here's how …

Stephen pressed play on his power point presentation and watched intently …

'Powerful thinking inspires a brave new world,' eulogised Stephen in the film, as the Translate Technology mantra emblazoned on his screen.

'This next clip will generate a few tears,' he thought, flippantly, as he observed the scene unfold.

He went back to his mirror and continued, 'The scene you have just watched testifies to my statement. The man in the clip - a father, brother, son, uncle and friend as you witnessed, was gravely ill. This man's indigenous town, like so many across the globe had no health or dental care. It had no doctors or dentists. These people's basic, human needs were not being met. In response to this travesty, GSW's charitable organisation, namely "Global Standard Saving the World" has equipped volunteer medics in this region with the Translate Technology device to give non-Global speakers instant access to medical care. And this is how we did it … .'

Stephen watched transfixed, as a clip showed the interaction between doctor and patient and how they could communicate because of his ingenuity. He fantasised about the day when he would stand, shoulder to shoulder, with the world's most renowned innovators, accepting the revered Global Peace Prize.

He continued practicing his speech, looking intently for grey hair strands as he spoke, 'Global Standard Saving the World. You have witnessed the Translate Technology doing its job by allowing people to communicate, resulting in a life being saved. The patient, using his

Mother Tongue, input his symptoms into the device which was translated into Global Standard enabling the doctor to give a diagnosis. This doctor was then able to treat the man. Of course, we will not always see an acute case like this. Sometimes it will simply be a minor disorder, a throat infection perhaps or just a common cold. But, for these people and thousands around the globe, just the very reassurance from a qualified medic is medicine itself. To repeat a point, this device truly embodies the adage "powerful thinking inspires a brave new world". Could someone please spare a tissue for the gentleman in the front row,' he imagined.

'Thank you,' he replied to his imaginary audience. 'Powerful thinking indeed inspires a brave new world. Access to Global Standard will not only secure better health care, but it will also open the world and make us one united family. It will empower people everywhere to obtain a better future; a future in which they can communicate with anyone with ease, a future where no one will be left behind. Global Standard and the translate technology will truly open doors to prosperity, to a time when everyone can receive equality of education and opportunity. This will be achieved through the Global Standard Education Portal accessible through the Wi-Fi technology inbuilt into the device. As we speak, my company is supplying, gratis, wireless fibre infrastructure that will enable access in the most remote areas to ensure that people globally, can use the device. Indeed, if you would be so kind as to reach underneath your seats, you will find such a device. In a moment, I will ask my Head of Communications to take to the stage and guide you through a demonstration. The machine has been designed with the youngest users in mind which GSW and the

GSPC anticipate will be children from just twelve months old.

Stephen pressed play once again and watched the pre-recorded demonstration by his Head of Communications. 'If you would like to hold the machine in your hand, right or left, whichever you prefer. Then, simply, power it up, in the same manner you switch on your mini pc.'

Stephen closed his eyes in delight as he heard the familiar copyrighted music that had become synonymous with the GSW translation device. It sent a tingle through his body. He couldn't wait to hear the jingle resonate in the hallowed building when hundreds of people would turn it on simultaneously. Imagining the GSW and GSPC "One Language, One Version, One Vision" motto, followed by his latest mantra "Powerful thinking inspires a brave new world" with the backing jingle clearly audible, filled him with a pride he never thought could exist in the human soul.

He opened his eyes and continued watching the presentation …

'The device assumes no prior knowledge of Global Standard so what the user will see first is a selection of countries' flags, listed by colour coded Mother Tongue zones, for example this continent has a purple hue. This island here, he tapped at the device with his finger, is blue. The user will choose the appropriate country and region and the machine will automatically select the correct language or dialect. This takes the user to the next "symbol level" which is quite simply, name and date of birth. This brings me to a unique feature regarding name. The machine is pre-programmed to select a Global Standard version of the user's Mother Tongue name; hence affording the person a new Global identity.' Stephen paused the clip and recalled the day he had the insight to change a person's identity by affording them a Global Standard nomenclature.

"There'll be no room for dialects," he remembered thinking, "not in speech or written form. I will be the one to convince world leaders that only Global names are appropriate."

At that time, his name change plan had been just an idea that had not come to fruition. But as Global Standard prospered and became more than just a convention amongst prominent supporters, Stephen's new name law, went hand in hand with his new language law. Stephen resumed the film and watched as his Head of Communications continued with his exposition.

'The date of birth is paramount to the next level. GSW and the GSPC have consulted with child development experts and linguists and the machine is programmed to upload age-appropriate data. The prototype we have here today is geared at educating a child practically from birth. However, for older Mother Tongue children and adults alike, who have yet to attain fluency and who currently account for a high percentage of users, they will be able to work through the levels in accordance with age and ability. The symbols are the first level. The learner, as they become more proficient, will earn points which will take them to the next tier. There is also a translate button, which enables the learner to input a Mother Tongue word for an instant interpretation. By pressing the audio symbol, the user will also hear the GS pronunciation and will be given opportunities to practise.

'Here, you will note that the speaker is articulating a Global Standard voice which is devoid of any regional accent. This pronunciation is the standard to which all Global Citizens will aspire. As Mr. Law commented in his earlier speech, Global Standard will be accent, dialect and colloquialism free. This will enable world-wide communication in one common language. The learner will know when they have arrived at the correct pronunciation as the audio button will "congratulate" them, allowing them to earn the relevant points and progress to the next level.

GSW and the GSPC, along with the Technology in Education Programme, are looking at long term instruction. We are seeking to educate Mother Tongue users, aiming to produce Global Standard communicators who will pass the Language Test, an examination that will acknowledge proficiency and automatically afford Global Citizenship. This device will stay with the learner until they graduate as Global Citizens. For those children who receive the device at birth, it will be their blueprint for education. It will be their development tool, their textbook, their life.

Of course, we appreciate that children learn at different rates. But the GSPC and GSW believe that if children and adults alike follow the programme, they will succeed and pass the language test. The more academically able will, irrefragably, complete the programme quicker. Furthermore, those children who finish the scheme early will be automatically awarded the prestigious title of "Global Standard Youth Language Ambassador". This role will enable the more gifted and talented to become peer mentors to the less academically able. It is intended that this will encourage the less capable to focus on their studies.

'So, moving on, the whole educational lifespan of the child will be stored on this device. The data is automatically saved to a main server at GSW headquarters so there is no need to worry about loss, damage or malfunction. Each device has biometric access and is licensed only to the user which ensures there's no identity fraud. GSW has a team of data analysts and computer security experts who will ensure that the mainframe is only accessed by those with special clearance. It has the following built-in features: Wi-Fi technology to enable the user to connect wherever they are in the world. As already mentioned, it has an audio button to perform the correct pronunciation of words. It also has a unique symbol function so the learner can navigate between topics, such as sports and hobbies.

To facilitate the Technology in Education Programme the device has two access options: the Learner feature, which I have already shown, and the Teacher option. It is the Teacher option that will enable the programme to succeed. The device has been pre-programmed with lessons in: Global Standard Language and Literature, Mathematics and the Sciences. Our extensively researched curriculum will provide schools with a lesson plan that will take pupils from pre-school to graduation. Our scheme has already received an endorsement from the Education Ministers in Global Motherland and the Sub Motherlands. In addition to this, the programme is currently being discussed by various country leaders who have adopted Global Standard as their official language, with a view to it becoming enshrined in their country's educational law.

Stephen closed his eyes and imagined he could hear the exuberance in the building with people praising his vision and foresight. He dreamt of a standing ovation in honour of his accomplishment, in tribute to his late father's original ideas.

'Now all I need is an invitation to the hallowed building,' he thought, positively, knowing that was just a matter of time.

12

'Jet black writing on a blood orange background sends out the message I want to convey,' barked Stephen austerely.

'But Sir, the white lettering against the background we discussed looks less … less … ,' responded Rod, sheepishly.

'Less what? Less effective? Less. Who wants less? Less says weak. Less says the flag stands for nothing,' retorted Stephen, sharply.

'Less menacing to the rest of the world. We do not want to appear a dictatorship,' murmured Rod, apprehensively.

'Rod, Rod, Rod,' muttered Stephen, patronisingly, just as he had the day he convinced Rod to renounce his Mother Tongue. Stephen perused the flag, the one he designed. The one he ensured looked threatening. Stephen's foresight that the flag would be a symbol to everyone that Global Standard is THE LAW meant that it had to evoke a tyrannical appearance. His plan for Global Standard was not merely a "sound business idea", as Norman had once blandly commented, but LAW, a new language law that country after country would embrace.

'Rod, I realise that you are not physically here and therefore cannot appreciate the material, workmanship and the way the flag will be displayed by a Language Monitor. I understand that a virtual view is not the same as seeing it in real life, but when the Language Monitors march into Area Blue and the GSW flag is hung in place of their ancestral flag you will, as my Language Warrior, be proud to march out and greet your Language Monitors. You will be proud to salute them in the name of Global Standard. And when the Education Minister in that area officially confronts that region's Minority Language Association and rejects his own ancient tongue in favour of Global Standard, you will be elated that we did not settle for less. You will be empowered in the name of Global Standard. And when that same Education Minister participates in a GSW Mother Tongue Renouncing Ceremony in the area's Parliamentary building, you will renege every thought and word regarding the diminution of the flag.'

'Yes, Sir,' said Rod, feeling grieved that his role was to follow orders, whether he agreed or not.

'Transfer me to the V.T.C.,' commanded Stephen.

Rod placed his mini p.c. on his desk, pressed the conference button which projected a widescreen image of Stephen and his surrounding office, onto his own wall.

'That's better,' said Stephen, who had the same widescreen experience as Rod.

'Now, sit down and listen,' instructed Stephen.

As Rod obeyed, he heard a commotion which seemed to be coming from outside Stephen's office, which, if he wasn't mistaken, sounded like marching. As Rod sat and waited, the noise became louder; it seemed like whatever was happening outside Stephen's office was about to replicate in his own office.

'Pay close attention,' Stephen repeated to Rod, as he left his chair and opened his office door.

Rod sat transfixed as two GSW employees, clothed in what he assumed was the Language Monitor's uniform that Stephen had covertly designed, marched in sync into Stephen's office. They stood still, expressionless, while another entered sporting the same costume and bearing the black and orange flag (Rod wondered why they had debated its colour when Stephen had already made the decision to proceed) expertly positioned in a body flag holder, which covered the anonymous marcher's face. They stood in a triangular pyramid of obedience.

'As you've no doubt deduced, this is the uniform that will be worn when we march into Mother Tongue Area Blue,' clarified Stephen. He continued, 'Notice how the pitch-black jacket and trousers match perfectly with the hue of the flag. This soft-shell material has been chosen as it is lightweight, waterproof, windproof, breathable and flexible; essential components that will keep a Language Monitor comfortable from dawn to dusk. This innovative material is supple enough to guarantee that the tie sits neatly underneath the shirt collar, whilst ensuring the gig line of a traditional military uniform is maintained,' explained Stephen. 'Next, note the detail on the shoulder pads. On the right lapel we have the newly patented GS symbol,' commented Stephen as he zoomed in on the hand-crafted badge with his pointer which enabled Rod to see how the 'S' coiled into the G, like a snug snake.

'The GS badge design, albeit slightly smaller, is replicated in the jacket buttons.' Stephen was now in full flow. 'On the left collar we have the recently designed and licensed LM symbol,' homing in once more. Rod noticed that the neon red that Stephen had chosen for each badge, matched perfectly with the "One Language, One Version, One Vision" signs that adorned the skyscrapers and the GSW and GSPC buildings. The GS and LM lapel badges were identical in dimensions and positioned in the same place on each lapel.

'So, moving onto the tie, which, I'm sure you'll agree, is the centrepiece of any uniform. For this part we are going to need the lights turned off,' said Stephen. He clapped his hands once authoritatively and the office plunged into near blackness enabling Rod to see why the dimness was needed. From his own office, Rod was able to see the position of the Language Monitors, who had maintained their motionless stance, because the GS and LM lapel badges, GS buttons and ties they were wearing were reflecting a neon red glow that was visible in the darkness. Stephen re-illuminated the room. 'These unique features will ensure that citizens are able to see the Language Monitors as they patrol, around the clock. This visibility will reinforce the Monitor's role which is to ensure that citizens are not conversing in any vernacular other than Global Standard. If any citizen is detained by a Monitor for breaking the new language law, he or she will bear the full consequences.' Stephen paused.

'Children under the age of fourteen will receive a suitable punishment,' he concluded. Rod waited in trepidation to hear what the punishment would be. His pulse quickened at the realisation that his own Mother Tongue would cause him conflicting emotions regarding enforcing this new directive. But to Rod's consternation, Stephen offered no explanation of the penalty and instead, continued his uniform expository. Rod unhappily acknowledged that what Stephen had set out to achieve in the name of Global Standard was coming to fruition. Stephen only had to utter a new decree and Rod became extremely anxious. Stephen's plans were becoming live.

'The socks, also bear the GS logo. The shoes are premium grade patent leather which ensures a highly polished appearance. Each Language Monitor will be given GS cufflinks which are to be worn always – I will not tolerate any excuse that they have been misplaced. The belt has a GS buckle and the clasp doubles as a flag holder, like so.' As Stephen signalled to the Language Monitor to give a demonstration of the dual-purpose belt buckle, Rod felt a heavy clamping pressure on his chest, that, as Language Warrior, he would be responsible for implementing this new law in a region of Motherland where its citizens were unaware that their lives were about to change forever. They had no idea that the hierarchy of their region had been bought.

Rod quickly refocused to see Stephen demonstrating how the GS tie should be worn universally. He looked on curiously as Stephen revealed a technique that Rod had been taught by his own father when a young child. It was the same knot that all his friends used, because they too had been taught by their fathers, grandfathers, uncles, brothers or cousins.

Rod was mystified why Stephen would go to the trouble of ensuring the Language Monitor dress code was equivalent to a military uniform, yet allow the most essential ingredient, the tie knot, to be an old- fashioned design mainly used by children. Rod's father referred to it as his Sunday knot, because their weekly visit to church as a family enabled him to wear this more relaxed style. It was a method Rod would never forget.

In fact, most mornings he had to stop himself from wearing his tie in such an informal manner, thinking that Mr. Law would disapprove and tell him to change it to a more business-like one. Rod scrutinised Mr. Law and the tie round his neck. He couldn't believe how he had never noticed before that he was employing the same style that Rod wanted to wear every day.

'Who would have taught Mr. Law this technique?' he mused. 'His grandfather? How could I have forgotten the old man?' He recalled the Global Standard launch day and his meeting with the elderly gentleman. Tactically, he thought, 'I still have the Mother Tongue grandfather card to play.' He reasoned that if implementing this plan in Area Blue became too difficult then he would somehow use this indiscretion to his advantage.

‘How touching his love for his grandfather would have such an impact all these years later. Does he even realise that this is not a military style knot? Should I tell him before someone else does?’ Rod pondered. As he deliberated his next move, he looked at the tie once more. As Stephen held it up to the magnifier facility on the projector, enabling Rod to have a close-up, he noticed there was a faint pattern on it that he recognised. It was a very subtle motif because it was the same colour as the tie, but one with which Rod was remarkably familiar because his father had owned a red paisley necktie with a similar pattern.

It was a replica of the tie that he had seen Stephen’s grandfather wearing on launch day. Rod was, of course, correct about the paisley garment, but was unaware that he had the identity of the grandfather completely wrong.

13

As Stephen continued his exposition, Rod sat exasperatedly at his desk. He didn't know how much more information he could take, but Stephen wasn't finished.

'Pay close attention,' he commanded Rod, once again. Rod sat upright in his chair, realising he had allowed himself to slump, ever so slightly, but sufficiently so that Stephen must have noticed.

Despite how inferior Stephen made Rod feel, he couldn't deny that he had accomplished a great deal. Irrespective of the future consequences for citizens in Area Blue, in some conflicting way Stephen's vision was to be respected. His conviction that Area Blue would be the "guinea pig" was about to become a reality. Stephen was a visionary in the truest sense of the word.

'Listen carefully to the rules of how the flag should be presented,' began Stephen.

Rod observed Stephen. His focus was almost unhuman. He hadn't missed a beat delivering the information. His eyes were blood shot and his face was so full of expression that Rod wondered how he was even catching his breath. For a slight moment Rod wanted to say to him, 'Stephen, breath, just breath … ,' but Rod knew better.

'The flag will be displayed at full mast on the GSW, GSPC and epicentre buildings day and night. It will also be exhibited strategically at other places within Global City, the Motherland, Sub Motherlands and those countries which have sworn allegiance to GSW. I have sent you and the Sub Leaders a map, which shows the precise locations. The after dark, neon red glow, demonstrated on the Language Monitor uniform, has been copied onto the flag. From dusk to dawn, this feature will ensure that the Global Standard motto is upheld in prominence and superiority.

Stephen continued, 'Whilst holding the flag, the bearer must make sure that the pole never touches the ground and that it is displayed correctly – that is, not the wrong way round. The flag should be held at a ninety-degree angle, ensuring that the bearer's face is not visible. This way the flag is always the centre of attention and not the flag holder. In addition to this … ,' Stephen stopped abruptly as Claudia, his secretary, entered the room. She whispered something into his ear, which resulted in him dismissing the Language Monitors, ordering them to "quick march", whilst ending his conference call with Rod immediately and without explanation.

Rod was flabbergasted that Claudia had not only entered Stephen's office without permission, whilst they were in the middle of a meeting, but that she had walked up to Stephen unperturbed and dared to approach him. Rod thought back to Joan and how, in all the time he had known her as Stephen's secretary, she had sat the other side of the glass, having no contact with him unless directly initiated by Stephen. Yet Claudia, whom Stephen had poached from the GSPC, seemed to have full access to him. She was completely comfortable in his presence, which was extremely odd. No one had access to Mr. Law. No one ever felt at ease. No one it would seem, except Claudia.

What she had discretely informed Stephen was the Secretary General was on the GS Select phone asking to speak with him immediately. The GS Select phone was an additional line of telecommunication that Stephen had specially installed. The contact number was only given to the honoured few. Since Claudia had been Stephen's secretary this phone had never rung. So when it started ringing, Claudia had, at first, been startled. Then she panicked because Mr. Law had instructed her to answer it within three rings. Not four or five, three. It had to be three. Claudia was grateful that the phone had been programmed with a long ring tone that lasted at least four seconds. After about eleven seconds she hastily picked up the receiver, relieved that the caller hadn't hung up.

'Yes, Sir. Right away. Please stay on the line,' she answered, courteously. Without hesitation, she calmly entered Stephen's office, walked up to him and whispered in his ear. Something she had never done before; something she would never have dreamt of doing usually. But she was aware that Mr. Law was desperately waiting for this phone call. She knew invading his personal space was a bold move. When he nodded and thanked her, she was as surprised as Rod, who watched, amazed. Rod in fact, jumped to the wrong conclusion, believing that Claudia and Mr. Law had an employer-employee relationship. He thought back to the launch party when Mr. Law had been amiable with his sister, Angelina. 'Now it would seem there are two people in the world with whom he engages normally,' thought Rod, pondering Stephen's behaviour.

14

Aphia and Grigor drove out of town and headed to the mountain village. The sun's yellow haze sat peacefully on the lake, like a cosy blanket. The fuzzy, orange tint reminded Grigor of the day he had met Aphia. He'd come to the lake to fish, not expecting to see anyone there at dawn, especially not someone who would become his wife. As Grigor pulled down the sun visa, the familiar backdrop of the lake reflected in the mirror, like a freeze-framed postcard.

The lake was filled with so many memories of his teenage years, diving and practising his fishing technique. Each time he fished, walked or drove past the lake, it seemed all his memories, happy and sad, were nestled at the bottom, and his very presence would send them cascading to the surface. As Grigor repositioned his mirror to protect his eyes from the glare, he was drawn to the background, to a bright orange glistening spark that appeared to be jumping in and out of the water. The orange glint seemed to be multiplying in its hundreds, as flashes upon flashes, reflected in his visa and side mirrors, causing him to reach for his sunglasses.

'There are fish in our part of the lake,' he muttered to himself, remembering the day when, as a teenager, he fled to the lake for solace, trying to alleviate the upset and anger he felt towards Nastan Popov for leaving town to study Global in the International School.

'There are fish in our part of the lake,' he repeated audibly, for some illogical reason, just like when he called out to Nastan that day.

'What?' laughed Aphia, bemused, 'what did you say about fish?'

Wondering why, yet again, his mind was reminiscing about Nastan, he dismissed his comments to Aphia as nothing more than childhood memories.

As they neared the mountain village, Aphia became overwhelmed by the lie her life had become. She did not know how she was going to pretend she was familiar with the area that Grigor believed had been her home for over four years. The only times she visited recently, were covertly, under the cover of darkness. When Grigor had been at town council meetings in the evenings, with the aid of a hand-drawn map from her father, she tried to find her way around the village. Aphia hoped these evening visits, aided by torchlight, would be enough to convince Grigor that this area had indeed been her home.

Grigor, himself, was familiar with the mountain because he had been there many times with Jakov. However, he had never met Aphia's grandmother. When Grigor became Jakov's clerk at eighteen years old, fresh from finishing school, he loved that his duties included accompanying Jakov on his community visits. Jakov always stressed to Grigor that the mountain folk needed as much attention, if not more, than the town folk. Jakov never neglected his duty to spend time with his mountain friends. For years, Jakov and Grigor had taken the same route which led them up the dirt track, past the cemetery and then another short walk to the numerous clusters of houses that were nestled neatly together in figure eight shapes that wound tightly out of sight.

'Who lives there?' Grigor had asked, curiously, on his first visit, pointing to a lone house that was set higher up the mountain, overlooking the town below.

'Nobody,' Jakov replied, subdued.

'But it looks so well kept. Somebody must live there,' Grigor insisted.

‘I can assure you, Grigor, nobody lives there,’ he replied, succinctly.

Jakov had been relieved that Grigor didn’t question him more about the solitary dwelling. He had been further grateful that he didn’t have to tell him about the “nobody” who lived in that house; a nobody who lived a secluded life in the mountain village all because of her atrocious comments that day in the museum. What she said was inexcusable, intolerable. Jakov would never be able to tell Grigor how the words of the language traitor who lived in that house caused the death of his dear Apollos. How her outspoken support for Global replacing their Mother Tongue sent Apollos early to his grave. Over the years Grigor never mentioned that day in the museum and Jakov had no intention of ever speaking of those events again. So when Jakov passed away, the knowledge of Aphia Joan’s outspoken support for Global died with him.

However, all these years later, unknown to Grigor, some mountain folk, in honour of Aphia Joan and her opinion that people should be free to learn and speak any language they desired, were speaking Global – albeit just conversationally. He had no idea that the Global language skills they acquired had been ignited by his wife’s grandmother. Her legacy in the mountain village was the advocacy of freedom of speech, that whoever wanted to learn Global, could and should. But it was something the mountain folk kept secret from Jakov; a clandestine way of life of which Grigor was also unaware. The new Mayor carried on the wishes of his predecessor and they knew that speaking it was still strictly forbidden. Every time Grigor visited, not one person spoke Global or revealed their language secret. Remarkably, Grigor had never ventured to the lone house, recalling Jakov’s words that nobody lived there. He had no idea that this house was where his Aphia was about to lead him.

Aphia closed her eyes to visualise the map. It was an easy route as the house was at the end of a straight incline that cut into the mountain side. But despite this, she was worried that she would get lost as she hadn't been there in daylight for such a long time. Aphia's eyes were still closed when the car came to an unexpected halt.

'Why have we stopped?' asked Aphia, curiously.

'What do you mean?' replied Grigor, bemused by her question.

'Why have you parked the car?'

'Because we're on foot from here, naturally. The road isn't big enough for a car. Are you quite okay?'

Aphia laughed, trying to cover her mistake.

Aphia looked at Grigor, burdened by yet more deceit.

'Ready?' suggested Grigor.

'Ready,' affirmed Aphia, closing her eyes once more, to picture the map. 'This way,' she said briskly and started walking up the track.

'This path also leads to the cemetery. Would you like to visit your grandmother's grave, Aphia?' asked Grigor, sympathetically.

Aphia stopped abruptly in her tracks as she realised that she had never seen her grandmother's grave. She died when Aphia was living in Global City and it was impossible for her to make the journey home. Her mother had later told her, that when people from town asked why she was not at the funeral, she told them that Aphia was unwell herself; that losing her grandmother had caused her too much anguish. Aphia hadn't understood why her parents felt it necessary to lie about her whereabouts.

She thought they were proud of her leaving home for a life in Global City. However, her mother had told her that, even though they had no problem with her leaving home, others would not understand. They would have judged Aphia and her parents for allowing her to go. So, the story Aphia thought she alone had fabricated, had also been the story her parents had told. They pretended Noadiah and Aphia were caring for their grandmother.

'Yes, I would like to,' responded Aphia, solemnly. 'We don't have to; if we continue straight ahead we'll bypass the graveyard,' said Grigor, caringly. He had never seen Aphia look so ghostly white. He took her by the hand and started to lead her away from the cemetery.

'It's okay, Grigor. I want to,' she said, yanking his arm, causing him to stop.

'Would you please go first,' asked Aphia.

'Of course,' replied Grigor, clasping her hand tightly. As Grigor led the way, Aphia felt overwhelmed with guilt at her manipulation of him. Yes, she genuinely loved him and yes, she was sincerely overcome with sadness about her grandmother, but she was equally concerned with how she had so easily used her despair, unknown to Grigor, to lead the way to a cemetery she had never visited before.

Aphia was surprised that the path leading to the cemetery was not overgrown but was paved with stones of all shapes and colours. It was like stepping into one of the fairy tales she had read as a child. This track did not resemble the unruly woodland nearby. It led to an oasis of peace and calm. The chaos of brambles on either side of the trail up to the mountain village was nowhere to be seen.

As Aphia allowed Grigor to direct her, she couldn't help but wonder why he didn't notice the rhododendron hedges of red, pink and white that laced the walkway; why he didn't stop to ask her if she could smell the honey-like aroma that overwhelmed her senses or if she could hear the bee-eater birds' sweet tunes oozing from deep inside the flowers. He seemed oblivious to it all.

As Grigor continued, Aphia noticed a large clearing to the left of the path which caused her stomach to fill with apprehension. Grigor suddenly felt her hand slip from his. He looked back to see her in a trance, staring vacantly at the way ahead; her complexion had paled further and she looked a ghastly grey. Her lips had tinged purple and she couldn't catch her breath. Grigor lovingly placed his hands on her shoulders and looked into her glazed eyes.

'It will be okay,' he reassured her, hoping his support would give her the courage she needed to persist. He took her hand again and pressed on to the clearing. Aphia wanted to turn and flee. She wanted to run back through the fairy tale path and not stop until the truth didn't matter. But the only place she felt like a lie was acceptable; the only place that people didn't care about such truths was Global City. She had run there once before. She wondered if she should again. As she turned her face away from Grigor and looked back, the fairy tale path began to disappear. Stone by stone, flower by flower, leaving nothing but brambles and thorns.

'Where's it all gone?' Aphia cried out. 'It can't have just disappeared. Where's it gone?'

Grigor looked at her in bewilderment, 'Where's what gone? We haven't reached the cemetery yet?'

'I don't mean the cemetery. Where are the flowers and birds? And the smell of honey?' she gasped, breathing in deeply through her nostrils. Grigor looked at her empathetically, not knowing or understanding what she meant. It was then Aphia realised the fairy tale path and its surroundings had never been there in the first place. That's why Grigor hadn't commented, that's why he hadn't turned to her and smiled. She realised they were only in her imagination.

She continued searching for the path, wishing that it would reappear. As she looked, longingly, she thought she saw someone in the distance, standing in the woods. An immaculately dressed man in a navy suit with a red paisley tie. He seemed so out of place amongst the wildness of the brambles and bushes. She looked intently trying to make out the features of his face but he was too far away.

'Aphia,' she heard Grigor calling softly. She turned and saw his outstretched hand beckoning her to come.

She looked back to the woods to see the impeccable stranger also with his hand extended towards her. She heard an authoritative voice calling, 'Joan, you belong with me. Joan … ,' which was interjected by Grigor's gentle tones, 'Aphia, whatever is wrong? You are worrying me.'

Her body swayed back and fore as in a tug of war, wanting to go to them both. She wanted to run to the immaculate stranger but did not know why. There was something familiar about him that gave her a sense of belonging. Both men were using her name; the stranger calling her Joan and her husband Aphia.

Joan, Aphia, Aphia, Joan, swirled around in her head. Joan, Joan Marsh, is that who I am? Aphia Joan Demas, my maiden name, is that who I am? Mrs. Grigor Saul - that's who I've promised to be forever,' she thought, pondering her wedding vows. As she wheeled once more in Grigor's direction, her eyes were drawn to the cemetery where her grandparents were buried. She saw her grandfather's headstone, his name in bold script carved into the granite "Agabus Demas, beloved husband of Aphia Joan Demas, a much-loved father and grandfather".

She hadn't thought about her grandfather in such a long time. She was just two years old when he died. It was as if he had never even existed. As Aphia stared at the gravestone, her grandmother's name evoked wonderful memories of love, reassurance and hope for the future. She looked at Grigor and realised that with him that love was manifest. She felt safe and accepted. She looked to the man who was now making his way through the woods towards them. As Aphia's eyes locked with his, she realised who he was. It was the grey-streaked hair she had not recognised. It was then she identified Stephen Law. She stared intently at him and shook her head dismissively. As she did, he retreated until he disappeared into the woods.

Feeling instantly released from Stephen, Global City and her old life she grabbed Grigor's hand.

'Can we please go home?' she pleaded longingly. Seeing that she was obviously distressed by the whole mountain experience he nodded silently and led her away from the cemetery. Aphia knew that she needed to tell Grigor the truth. She knew that their life together could not be layered like this with lie after lie.

15

Georgia heard muffled voices coming from outside. The bedroom window was slightly ajar, which enabled her to listen to Norman and Linda conversing in their Mother Tongue. Their soothing resonances reminded her of the first morning she had woken up in their home and how her laboured sleep had prohibited her full consciousness.

At that time, Norman and Linda's foreign words floated around the room, depositing themselves in Georgia's sleepy ears causing her confusion and dismay because she could not understand them. She believed her sea voyage had taken her to Global City, where everyone spoke Global. As Georgia's consciousness slowly peeped through and the realisation of her strange surroundings had set in, she frantically spurted question after question at Norman and Linda in her Mother Tongue. But, she soon realised this man and woman, whoever they were, did not understand what she was saying.

'Where am I?' she had asked over and over in her Mother Tongue.

As Linda and Norman continued to respond in their language, they had been concerned about Georgia's distressed state.

'You're going to be just fine,' Linda said, reassuringly, again and again. As Georgia drifted back into the comfort of sleep, despite her best efforts to stay awake, she thought she heard Norman and Linda speaking Global. It was a strange type of Global which was a mixture of Global words that she recognised and their own language. This language switching made it possible for Georgia to understand fragments of what they were saying, and this made her believe that she was in Global

City after all. Frantically, Georgia blurted as many Global words as she possibly could. They had no idea that Georgia's intended destination was Global City. For their part, Norman and Linda had been flabbergasted that Georgia was miraculously able to converse with them in a shared language.

But now, as Georgia continued listening to Norman, Linda and this stranger communicate in their own language she felt concerned that their words were frantic, harsh and rushed. Georgia could not understand what they were saying but she knew from the tone of their voices it was a disagreement. There was a lot of repetition of one word that Georgia concluded was "no" because as Norman said it, he also used his body to stop the stranger entering their home. Georgia deduced that the unwanted visitor was a policeman as the uniform mirrored that of the police officers in her own country. The man's words were short and sharp, and then he departed. Norman and Linda retreated and hurriedly closed their front door.

Feeling fearful that the heated conversation was because of her presence in their home, Georgia made her way to the landing and crept down the stairs hoping that she would be able to overhear Norman and Linda's conversation. Georgia stood motionless on the bottom stair deciding that if they caught her listening she would pretend she was coming down for breakfast. Georgia could hear their worried voices coming from the kitchen.

'We should have realised we couldn't carry a body from the beach and think no one noticed,' ranted Norman.

'We haven't done anything wrong,' Linda reassured him.

'That's obviously not how the community are seeing it. He'll be back you know and the next time we will have no choice but to let him in to search for Georgia. I don't understand how those parents from the beach that day knew it was us. Did you recognise anyone? The children were so young I didn't know any of them. Did you?' asked Norman, feeling sceptical that their allegiance with Global had caused someone in their village to go telling tales as retribution. This potential act of treachery made him feel incredibly irate.

'We carried a dishevelled body through the village and back to our home. If it wasn't the people from the beach then anyone could have seen us,' said Linda, logically.

'The others who washed up on shore further down the coast cannot communicate with the police. I'm assuming they speak Georgia's native tongue and possibly Global the same as Georgia. But of course no one in our village will speak Global with them, despite there being many Global speakers, so they won't have a common language in which to talk.'

'They have a duty to look after them despite where they come from. Food, water, shelter and clothing should not be determined by language; it's a basic human right. They must be terrified,' said Linda, recalling how frightened and fragile Georgia was when they had found her.

'Why do you think they are so intent on finding her?'

'I don't know. The missing jigsaw piece maybe?'

'Well we must protect her. We must protect them all,' said Norman, emphatically.

Georgia crept back upstairs completely frustrated that the very time she needed Norman and Linda to speak Global, they didn't utter a word. She wept silent tears for her friends, not knowing if they were alive.

16

Realising that she was stranded here indefinitely unless she opened-up to Norman and Linda, Georgia decided that she needed to know her location. She needed to know how far she had travelled from her homeland and if she was anywhere near Global City. She needed to know if she was the only survivor from her voyage or if her friends had also washed up on shore. She prayed that they had and was anxious to find out. Also, she longed to see her sister, Phoebe.

Norman and Linda were busy discussing the morning's events in raised whispers. Georgia felt like screaming at them that she didn't understand a word they were saying so stop with all the whisperings.

Georgia assumed because Norman and Linda were speaking another language that she was miles away from Global City. She had no idea that Area Blue was a region within Global Motherland and that she was about a three-hour drive from her intended terminus.

Her sudden appearance caused Norman and Linda to stop talking.

'How are you?' asked Linda. 'Homesick,' said Georgia, pitifully.

'Poor lamb. Sit and I'll make some tea,' said Linda. 'I think bits are coming back to me,' said Georgia. 'That's wonderful,' said Norman. 'What can you remember exactly?'

'A boat. I can remember a boat and my friends. We are smiling. We are so happy; we are going on an adventure.'

'That's good, anything else?' asked Norman, quizzically.

‘It’s a beautiful day and we are at the beach. It looks a lot like your beach and we are running to the sea. We get into a plastic … I’m not sure how you say the word properly, a dinghy? I think it’s the first time we have done this because we are wearing life jackets for safety. Then we start singing and paddling. We are so happy,’ she finished, solemnly.

As Linda listened intently, Norman asked, ‘So you were at the beach just enjoying a day out? What happened next?’

‘A storm. A terrible storm: the sky is black. And the rain, I have never seen rain like it. The boat is dragged out by the tide and we start floating away from the shore. We are paddling and paddling to get back to land but the force of the wind is too strong. The waves take us further and further away and then the lightning starts. We are so scared at this point and huddle together. We start singing, louder and louder to drive away the fear. But the louder we sing, the stronger the wind becomes. We stop singing and that’s it, that’s all I can remember,’ said Georgia, making the experience sound like an accident that she had drifted from her homeland.

‘That would make sense,’ said Norman pulling out a map. ‘We are here,’ he said. ‘These countries are across the channel but the language they speak is not yours which makes it harder to figure out where you come from. Can you remember the name of your Mother Tongue? That would help us a lot.’

‘I’m sorry, no,’ replied Georgia, transfixed with the map, as her eyes tried to search out Global City. But what she didn’t know was the map Norman had, was years old and the Motherlands and Global City didn’t even exist when it was printed.

Georgia needed to probe further. 'It's a shame I can't remember the name of my language or my hometown. It would make it so much easier for me to go back. I have nothing, no passport, mobile phone, money. I have nothing,' she repeated, dolefully.

'You don't need to worry about anything. You may stay here as long as it takes to figure things out,' said Norman, looking anxiously at Linda, knowing that the authorities were due to call at any time and that he did not have a plan B.

'Unless,' he said, unexpectedly 'unless we take Georgia to Global City and she can stay in our house there until we find a way to send her home,' he said to Linda, animatedly.

'Have you lost your mind, Norman? You can't return to Global City.'

'Why not? I'm on bereavement leave. I didn't resign, remember?' he said to her rolling his eyes.

'What is Global City? I thought this was your home but you have another?' asked Georgia, enthralled and in disbelief that Norman was actually considering escorting her to the very place she wanted to be.

'Global City is in this country and yes we have a house there. It is the "so called" Global Standard capital of the Motherlands,' said Norman, deep in thought.

'What is Global Standard?' asked Georgia, not realising why she was concerned by that term.

'It's the new version of the Global language. It's being enshrined into law superseding all other Global formats. Every Global Citizen will now have to speak this alternative form or else!'

'Norman, you will scare the child, speaking about Global City like it is some kind of gated prison,' scolded Linda.

‘You said it!’ replied Norman, cynically.

Georgia quickly processed the sinking fact that since learning Global it had been usurped by a new variant.

‘So is the new way of speaking Global hugely different from the old?’

‘It depends what version people have been speaking. For Motherland citizens there is no change. For Sub Motherland residents it’s just a few spelling corrections, really, to make it uniform. One language, one version, one vision,’ scoffed Norman, irately.

Georgia felt very uneasy about Norman’s disdain towards Global and Global City.

‘So, Georgia, how do you feel about staying in Global City for a while until we can get you home? People are asking questions about you around here and it’s probably better that you leave. Our house in Global City is in a quiet suburb and you could stay there without the worry of the authorities looking for you,’ explained Linda, trying to mask Norman’s hostility.

‘But what about my friends? Is there any information about them?’

Norman looked at Linda and nodded his head. ‘It’s excellent news. They have been found. The police came here this morning to let us know that they, like you, washed up on shore, wounded but alive. They are being looked after.’

‘Can we all go to this Global City? Can my friends come too?’

Norman looked at Linda again, knowing that the only way this could happen was if they liberated them from their place of confinement and covertly escorted them to Global City. This thought filled Norman with glee as he pondered how incensed Stephen Law would be if he knew of his plans.

Of course, he had no intention of notifying Stephen but just the thought of housing "illegals", as Stephen referred to them, gave him so much satisfaction. Norman recalled how Stephen had previously issued a directive that all GSPC employees were to be scrutinised to ensure their status in Global City was legitimate. Norman racked his brain to think how he could ensure more illegals came to the city.

'I wonder how many more friends Georgia has waiting on her command to make the journey,' he mused, certain that her voyage was for that very purpose and not what she had implied. 'I'll give her some time to settle into city life and then I will insist on the truth,' he thought, shrewdly. He remembered his words to Linda, "It will mean acting out of character for both of us," realising that his metamorphosis had begun.

Norman also recollected his words to Stephen that day in his office when Stephen had questioned why Area Blue had not renounced Mother Tongue in favour of Global Standard, in line with all Global speaking regions. "You are not the law. Global is not law. People are still free to speak whatever language they choose," he recalled telling him. "You have to remember that you are the leader of the FREE Global world. You are not an autocrat or a king. You are simply an entrepreneur with a superb business plan that is drawing more attention than I ever dreamed possible," he had continued. "I cannot override an official first language, which has been a medium of instruction for centuries; I cannot do it. It is not within my power."

Norman's words that day had incensed Stephen to ensure that his plans would become LAW. Norman had no idea that the globalisation of Area Blue had already begun and within twenty-four hours the Language Monitors would be at his seaside town, and all other locations within the area, gathering Mother Tongue citizens for participation in the first ever Mother Tongue renouncing ceremony.

Norman reiterated steadfastly to himself, 'Stephen Law is NOT the law. He doesn't have the authority to deport anyone! I will make my Global City home a haven for those who want to use it,' he enthused, pleased with how his thought processes were panning out. However, he was oblivious to the fact that his comment about Stephen NOT being the law couldn't be further from the truth.

'You stay here and be my alibi,' Norman told Linda.

'But what if P.C. Evans calls again? What am I to tell him?'

'Don't worry about him, he'll be miles away, investigating the sighting of a certain young female that he is so keen to speak with.'

'What do you mean?' asked Linda. 'And how are you going to get the others out of the detention centre?'

'Don't worry, just trust me. Being around David and Stephen Law has taught me how to be resourceful if nothing else.'

So Linda agreed to stay while Norman and Georgia drove to the Detention Centre. Georgia lay low on the back seat of the car under a blanket while Norman, under the cover of darkness and incognito broke in and freed Georgia's friends. One benefit of living in a town where there was hardly any crime was that there was never more than one police officer on duty. The one officer that was, had been chasing his tail for the last few hours, acting on an anonymous tip off searching for a mysterious young woman.

Norman knew that his actions were illegal but when he witnessed the reunion of Georgia and her friends, their cries and hugs at the very sight of each other and the realisation that they were all still alive, his out of character behaviour was worth every second.

He would get them to Global City as he had promised and would deal with the consequences of his actions as and if necessary.

17

'Who's there?' Claudia had queried hesitantly, seeing the blinds flicker in Norman's office. 'If Stephen Law has turned up once more uninvited … if he's sat at Norman's desk, like he runs the GSPC, he is about to find out that I do not hold him in any form of esteem. I am not one of his minions that hang on his every word. I am not Joan Marsh and I never will be … or want to be for that matter,' she thought defiantly, opening Norman's office door abruptly. But curiously, no one was there. Mr. Law was nowhere in sight. Unlike the day when Norman's father had died and Stephen barged straight passed Claudia into his office.

As she stood by the door, the blinds started to swish slightly and Claudia felt a cold breeze. She stretched to reach the handle and closed the window. As she secured the lever she noticed a reflection in the glass. A tall figure, a man, dressed in black. She swung round nervously but still, nobody was there. Her heart pounded, hoping her mind was playing tricks. She looked at the sofa that was just a few feet away. She was still unsettled about Norman's father's death. She adjusted the blinds back to their rightful place and a pang of sadness engulfed her as she thought of Norman, the dear man with whom she loved working. She had no idea when, or even if, he would return from his bereavement leave.

She hurried past the settee, feeling silly that she could still visualise the old man lying there, dead. She had met Norman's father many times and he was just as affable as his son. In fact, on many occasions Claudia kept him company when he turned up unexpectedly, causing Linda and Norman concern for his whereabouts.

But whenever his mind believed he was a young man again working in the city, he arrived like clockwork at Norman's office, safe and sound. She knew his illness made him confused but it never stopped him from chatting and laughing with her.

'Look sharp,' he'd say to Claudia, as he marched studiously passed her desk into Norman's office. If Norman wasn't there, he would call to Claudia, 'I'm ready to dictate a letter,' believing Claudia was his secretary. Of course, if Norman was in his office, it was the usual panic phone call to Linda to reassure her that he was free from harm. Norman knew exactly how to deal with his father. Claudia, too, had learned how to pacify him which kept him content until Norman came. Sometimes that meant sitting and taking minutes of a bogus letter he would dictate, believing it to be reality. Claudia found it fascinating listening to him spurt off instructions to colleagues and companies that he had so obviously engaged with during his working life.

Claudia closed Norman's office door, not wanting to leave it open for uninvited guests. As she sat at her desk she observed an envelope addressed to her. She looked around, wondering who had left it and when? She hadn't noticed it there a few minutes before. As she scrutinised it, she saw a reflection in the window behind her, the same dark, eerie shadow that she'd seen in Norman's office. Then, quite unexpectedly she heard a noise, a high-pitched scraping, a sound that she hadn't heard before which seemed to be coming from the lift.

'Hello. Who's there?' she called out, hoping someone could provide an explanation for the eerie din, but no one answered.

She looked at her switchboard and saw that David's telephone light was illuminated which meant he was engaged in a phone call.

'David must have left this while I was in Norman's office,' she deduced, perplexed why he would be sneaking around.

She opened the envelope and began to read, but the document inside didn't make sense.

"Secretary to Mr. Stephen Law". Then she saw her name, job title, salary, commencement date. She realised she was reading an employment contract; her employment contract at GSW.

Claudia placed the document on her desk, dazed by the unexplained job offer. As she sat, pondering the situation, her computer alerted her to an internal email from David that said:

"Dear Claudia,

Thank you for your transfer request, which I have accepted. May I wish you every success in your new role at GSW."

Feeling nonplussed and angry and knowing that David was still engaged in his phone call, she decided to go to his office to clarify the situation as she most definitely hadn't submitted a transfer request to GSW. As Claudia stood waiting for the lift, the disturbing, high pitched noise returned. The lift light indicated it was due to arrive and the awful noise stopped. Wondering if the elevator was faulty and if she would have to endure the racket whilst inside, she considered taking the stairs. As she backed away undecided, the lift doors opened abruptly.

Claudia was taken aback as she saw two boxes with her name clearly marked in black ink. Claudia entered the lift and pressed the hold button. The box lids hadn't been sealed which enabled her to open them with ease. She looked in the first which contained her personal belongings from her office drawers. She couldn't fathom when they had been emptied and by whom. Dismayed, she looked in the second box to find her cup and saucer, cutlery, sugar, tea and coffee jars, plastic bowls and the GSW carrier bag that she had kept from the GS launch day.

Enraged that David could be so dismissive and that he obviously had no intention of trying to talk her out of the fictitious request, she hit the hold button to release the lift and selected David's floor. But, instead of moving upwards, the lift dropped to the ground, accompanied by the same unsettling eerie tone. As the doors opened Claudia felt unnerved and confused by what had just happened. She wished that Norman was there to defend her, to take care of things. Worry and dismay sat in the pit of her stomach. Claudia stood in the lift gazing at the foyer of the GSPC. The security guard noticed her and thought she was behaving oddly.

'Are you okay Miss?' he asked.

Claudia looked at his benevolent face which bore the same expression day after day.

'I'm fine thank you,' she replied as she stooped down to collect her belongings.

Unquestioningly and accepting her fate, she headed directly to GSW to secure her job as secretary to the leader of the free Global world. It seemed that she would be Joan Marsh, after all.

18

'Mr. Secretary-General,' said Stephen respectfully.

'This is the P.A. to the Secretary-General,' replied the disembodied voice on the line.

'I am instructed to inform you that you may deliver your Global Standard presentation to the associate countries on the twenty first of August. Etiquette instructions will be emailed to your secretary immediately. Please ensure you read the information carefully and comply with protocol. The Secretary-General would like to stress that the decision to proceed with your proposal will be voted on by the associate countries themselves and not by the Secretary-General. Good day.'

Stephen listened to the monotone receiver, feeling slightly peeved that the Secretary General had not phoned himself, to invite Stephen to the hallowed building. In addition to this, the P.A., whom Stephen held in no higher esteem than Claudia, hung up the phone without even waiting for confirmation of acceptance.

'The twenty first of August. The twenty first of August,' sighed Stephen. 'Why are all the significant events in my life tied to this date? This birthday, I will ensure there is no surprise birthday cake and no Norman with his annoying phrases,' he grumbled, wondering where indeed Norman was. Not that he had missed him; things had been running fine without him.

Stephen had yet to meet Norman's superior but meeting him face to face wasn't important. All of Stephen's requests had been actioned; even poaching Claudia.

Admittedly, David had been surprised when Stephen had requested Claudia personally. He had been even more flummoxed when she'd left the GSPC suddenly, without working out any notice; particularly as Claudia seemed to detest Stephen. David recalled how appalled she'd been by his behaviour after the death of Norman's father.

19

Stephen Law stood proudly on the podium, gazing at his audience. Today was his birthday. From this day forward sharing this day with death ceased. His surroundings and onlookers confirmed that he had reached the pinnacle of his ambition. From today, his life began again.

'Ladies and Gentlemen. I am Stephen Law, Founder and CEO of Global Standard to the World. I am truly honoured to have been invited to this hallowed building which has hosted some of the world's greatest visionaries. I am humbled to share with you my vision for taking Global Standard to the ends of the earth … .'

Rod watched live on his mini pc from Mother Tongue Area Blue as Stephen began his address to the world's leaders. Stephen had a device, the size of a pin head, attached to his jacket lapel that ensured his presentation was recorded and simultaneously live streamed to Rod. Stephen began his exposition outlining reasons why the leaders should embrace Global Standard as the one common language of the world instead of their own Mother Tongues. Rod watched doubtingly. Despite Stephen's fervour for his vision, Rod was convinced that any endorsement of this legislation went against every individual human rights law that had ever been written. Imposing a language on people simply was not acceptable. Rod knew Stephen had already gained the validation of several world leaders who were present, but a few was simply not enough. He needed everyone's support.

'Powerful thinking inspires a brave new world,' eulogised Stephen as the video clip ended. 'Please, someone spare a tissue for the man in the front row,' he requested, stunned that his own vision had come true.

Rod looked on in disbelief that a prominent world leader was allowing his emotions to be on public display. He watched fearfully as Stephen convinced these powerful people that his plan for Global Standard was ethically correct and he saw the satisfaction on Stephen's face as he introduced his Head of Communications; someone whom Rod had never met.

He began, 'If you would like to hold the device in your hand, right or left, whichever you prefer. Then, simply, power it up in the same manner that you switch on your mini pc.' Stephen closed his eyes in delight as he waited to hear the familiar copyrighted music that had become synonymous with the GSW translation device. It sent a tingle through his body. The wait had been worthwhile as the jingle resonated throughout the building, just as he had envisioned. As the tune finished, Stephen looked at the screen that displayed the GSW and GSPC "One Language, One Version, One Vision" motto, followed by his latest visionary statement "Powerful thinking inspires a brave new world". He was yet again enveloped with a pride he never thought could exist in the human soul.

Rod watched as the world leaders seemed transfixed by the information and technology. They appeared equally as mesmerised by Stephen himself. As Stephen brought the presentation to a conclusion, those world leaders who had derided his plans stood up and began applauding stridently. Eventually, each world premier joined in the standing ovation in honour of Stephen Law. As Rod observed in disbelief that Global Standard had gained the backing of every single leader in the room, he noticed just one lone figure that hadn't stood to his feet and was not clapping. This man, who was dressed in black, sat motionless, staring at Stephen Law intently. Then, he stood up and left so swiftly that Rod was unable to see his face. Rod felt spooked by this brooding presence. He was puzzled whether he was for or against Stephen.

As Stephen left the podium and made his way down the aisle, passing the principals and presidents who were queuing to shake his hand, Stephen lowered his chin to his jacket lapel and said, smugly, 'Rod, Rod, Rod; that's how you gain the world. Tell the Education Minister in Area Blue that I no longer need his permission to eradicate his Mother Tongue because I just shook hands with his Prime Minister. Prepare to advance in the name of Global Standard.'

Rod removed his earpiece perturbed as he watched Stephen exit the building like a luminary, distressed that now there seemed nowhere to hide from him. He was everywhere. Suddenly, realisation dawned that the grandfather card Rod had planned to use as his get out clause, seemed weak. Rod concluded that his idle threat would be swallowed up in the vastness of who Stephen Law had just become.

20

Norman decided to stay overnight with Georgia and her friends to help them settle in. He phoned Linda who was relieved they had made it to Global City safely. She was looking forward to Georgia and her friends returning to their homes and then they could finally sell their Global City house and that would be that. Stephen Law, David and the GSPC would be behind them.

Norman fell asleep feeling pleased with all he had accomplished that day. He had freed Georgia's friends, reunited them and ensured they had a safe place to stay in Global City. He felt ashamed that it had taken Georgia's entry into their lives to remind him of his vow to Linda that as long as he was the GSPC Director, he would do everything in his power to stop the spread of Global Standard in Area Blue. The following morning, wearing his best suit, he would go to GSW and inform Mr. Law that he was returning to work. He would arrive unannounced as Stephen had done the day he marched into his office when his father had died. But he would be playing a game.

Norman would pretend to Stephen that he was sorry for not fully supporting him previously, blaming this on his grief. He would tell him that he was ready to return to work and he would support his Global Standard vision, no matter what. He knew this would appeal to Stephen's ego and he would be none the wiser about Norman's plan to ensure that Global Standard never, ever, replaced his ancestral language in Area Blue. The first thing he would achieve as GSPC Director would be to relieve Rod Jones of his duties in Area Blue, persuading Stephen that Rod's skill set was better suited to life in Global City.

Additionally, he would tell Stephen that this time round, he would engage with the Education Minister. He would convince him to accept Global Standard as the only language in Area Blue. Norman would then set himself up in his homeland under the guise of working in the best interests of GSW and the GSPC. But, he would do everything in his power to halt the spread of Global Standard.

As Norman approached the GSW building he wondered if his pass was still active and if he would have access to the building as before. Hesitantly he swiped his GSPC identity card and to his surprise the glass doors opened which allowed entry into the foyer area. A second swipe and another set of glass doors, allowed him into the building. The security guard greeted him amicably and Norman entered the lift. He pressed the button for the executive floor and the lift started moving swiftly. Norman got out but realised that he had mistakenly disembarked on the wrong level. As he deliberated whether to climb the stairs or re-enter the lift, he heard a sweet voice ask,

'Can I help you?' he turned and couldn't believe his eyes.

'Georgia? What are you doing here? Did you follow me?'

The young lady looked alarmingly at Norman.

'Georgia, do you think I am Georgia? Georgia is my sister. Who are you?'

Norman looked in disbelief at this young woman who was the exact replica of Georgia.

'Where are you from?' he quizzed. 'Originally, I mean. There's no need to pretend. If you are an illegal citizen then I can protect you. Your sister is safe, along with her friends in my home in the city.'

Phoebe was flummoxed. She could not declare that she was an illegal, especially in the GSW building and to a stranger with an unknown agenda.

'Sorry, I do not know what you mean, I was confused,' she retorted, walking away, concerned that Mr. Law was watching.

'Please, let me help you. Your sister needs you. This is my address,' said Norman hurriedly walking after her. 'You will find your sister and her friends here,' thrusting a business card in her hand. They can stay as long as they need.' She unwillingly took the card, not wanting to draw any more attention to their conversation.

'Is Mr. Law in the building?' Norman asked.

'Yes, he's always in the building,' she replied, 'especially today, of all days.'

'Why, what's today?' 'I have to go,' she said.

'What's today?' he asked, concerned.

'That,' said Phoebe, pointing to a monitor which showed live coverage of the activity in Area Blue. 'Globalisation is imminent, which will make Area Blue a Global Standard region.'

Norman looked on in horror as he watched the Language Monitors marching towards the Area Blue town square.

'What's happening there?' he asked, frantically.

'A Mother Tongue renouncing ceremony,' she replied, patriotically.

'Go to your sister,' Norman commanded Phoebe as he ran to the stairwell and fled the building.

He phoned Linda. 'Norman where are you? I have been ringing you non-stop. You need to come home immediately,' uttered a distraught Linda.

Stephen Law watched Norman on his security device. He particularly liked how flummoxed Norman had become when Phoebe alerted him to the carnage in Area Blue.

'Well, well, well,' said Stephen out loud. 'Aren't you looking chipper,' he continued sarcastically. 'What are you up to now my old friend …?'

He rewound the footage and listened to their conversation while Norman fled the building.

***

The three hour drive home seemed endless. As Norman passed Area Blue's town square he couldn't believe the carnage. He parked by the police station and watched as his fellow citizens looked like lost sheep, doing as they were told but not knowing why. His phone rang.

'Where are you?' whispered Linda in a querulous tone.

'I've just parked by the police station.' 'Are you at home?' asked Norman.

'No, I'm in a queue. People in uniform came to the seaside and rounded us up like criminals.'

'What are you queuing for?' asked Norman confused.

'I don't know,' said Linda, scared.

'Linda, get out of the queue and come to the Police Station.'

'I don't know if I can.' 'Can what? Leave?'

'Yes, other people have tried but the people in uniform won't let them.'

Knowing Linda must be referring to the uniforms he'd seen on the GSW monitor, he stated clearly, 'Linda, they have no real authority. This is all of Stephen Law. They can't make you stay. Just leave, now, this minute and meet me at the Police Station. Linda, Linda …?' the line went dead.

He dialled her number – no answer.

Norman was dumbfounded by what he was witnessing in his hometown. He pondered how on earth Stephen Law had orchestrated this unlawful legislation which seemingly was being reinforced by the region's Prime Minister. He heard David's words echo in his mind, "Didn't someone once say that convention is practically the same as law. I believe he will stop at nothing to achieve his goal." Norman recalled further how he had told Stephen that his idea for Global Standard was nothing but a sound business deal and he could not change language legislation in Area Blue.

"You are simply an entrepreneur with a superb business plan that is drawing more attention than I ever dreamed possible. We cannot force a region or non-Global speaking country to adopt Global Standard. Global Standard is not the law."

'Global Standard is not the law, Global Standard is not the law,' repeated Norman frantically not knowing what to do as it seemed that Global Standard was very much "the law". Then he remembered who he was and for whom he worked.

'Make way,' he barked, showing his GSPC identity. 'I'm looking for one language traitor in particular,' he announced officially to the Language Monitors.

'She's been harbouring illegals. I need to take her into custody. There she is,' he said, feeling relieved that he had spotted Linda. The Language Monitors had no idea she was his wife.

Norman walked over to her, 'Come with me,' he ordered authoritatively, grabbing her by the arm.

They walked away in silence, Norman showed his credentials to the Language Monitors as they left, reiterating her status as traitor.

They reached Norman's car.

'What next?' asked Linda, scared and in tears.

'Back to Global City,' said Norman, conscious of the irony that this was the safest option until they knew what was going on. He realised with frightening clarity that his plan to stop the spread of Global Standard and Stephen Law was way too late.

21

As Norman and Linda were escaping Area Blue, their ancestral friends were being rounded up like sheep in a pen. As people were forced to queue to enter the Parliamentary building, they were given a leaflet which explained the situation. Additionally, people began to receive message alerts simultaneously to their mobile devices. Area Blue citizens were perplexed, wondering how they were receiving this notification. No one recalled giving permission.

The propaganda styled edict, cited quite simply, two choices. The first, renounce Mother Tongue in favour of Global Standard which affords Global Citizenship, the right to work and live in the Sister Motherland and, for those whose Global needs improving, free Global Standard language lessons. In addition to this, all converted citizens will receive a standard issue mini pc which will enable them to fully integrate with other Global Citizens, receive news alert, messages from Stephen Law himself and afford them the freedom to travel between districts as their biometric information is also stored on the device.

Or option two, reject the new Global Standard language law and be labelled. The second option bears the consequence of expulsion from the Sister Motherland and deportation to the GSW holding centre where language traitors are detained until they convert to the Global Standard belief system.

As Norman and Linda travelled into the night they did not hear the cries from some of their friends as they bore the pain and humiliation of being “labelled”. They were unaware that Stephen Law had prepared a place for all the labelled. Neither did they see the construction of the furnaces that will burn and destroy all Mother Tongue literature, in print or digital, day and night, until there are no more to be found.

22

Linda had never felt so glad to be going to Global City. It was only because of Norman's stubbornness to resign his post as GSPC Director that he'd been able to liberate her from Area Blue.

'What on earth is that?' said Norman as they approached Global city. 'That wasn't there when I left earlier,' he observed.

'What are they?' Linda enquired, referring to the portable style huts that were paving the left side of the road.

'Search me,' replied Norman, completely puzzled.

As they approached the newly constructed barrier and guard hut, a Language Monitor appeared and motioned for them to drive into the first parking space. He then ordered them to produce their Global Citizen identity cards and exit the vehicle. As Norman and Linda handed over their IDs for inspection, another Language Monitor commanded them to step into one of the freestanding booths. Norman was so relieved that Linda had the foresight to bring her Global I.D. when she was taken from their home.

'I'll go first,' said Norman, not knowing the purpose of the booth. As he stood inside, a pre-recorded message told him to stand with his feet apart and raise his arms, palms upwards. As he obeyed, a red beam scanned his fingers, hand and wrist. Then, the disembodied voice instructed him to exit, whilst thanking him for his cooperation. Norman did not know the purpose of the machine but he indicated to Linda that it was okay, so she entered one also, for the scanning process.

As Norman was waiting for Linda to emerge, the first Language Monitor hurried over to him and said, 'Sir, my apologies, I did not realise your position within the GSPC. Please be on your way.'

Flabbergasted and lamenting that if he'd acted with authority upon reaching the checkpoint, he could possibly have saved them being scrutinised and subjected to the machine.

'Thank you. I'm glad to see the machine is working as planned. Has anyone questioned its purpose?' asked Norman, quite naturally.

'No, Sir and we are under strict instructions not to divulge its actual purpose to citizens.'

Norman needed to know its "actual" purpose but could not ask outright, because as GSPC Director he should be in possession of this knowledge already.

'Of course, if citizens ever find themselves in an ultraviolet light they will probably see their label,' the Language Monitor divulged.

'Do you have such a light? We can check my label to make sure things are in working order,' said Norman, not knowing what the label was.

'Certainly, Sir, you will have to go back into the booth for the label to be visual,' said the Language Monitor obligingly. Norman wondered if the Monitor believed he carried as much clout as Stephen and thought that his helpful attitude would earn him a commendation or a good word back to Stephen Law.

Intrigued, Norman stepped back into the booth and held out his hands.

'Turn your hands over please, Sir,' he instructed. As he shone his ultraviolet light onto his hands, Norman was horrified by what he saw. Imprinted on both his palms was a GS symbol. It was neon red in appearance and the S clamped into the G like a snug snake.

'Genius,' exuded Norman, trying to mimic a smile whilst feeling sick to his core. He wanted to rescue Linda from the booth and this tyrannical labelling but he knew this would not end well if he did.

'Indelible too,' the Language Monitor further commented, whilst Norman frantically resisted rubbing or scratching the label to check it's permanency.

'It's remarkable how Mr. Law has pioneered the first of its kind; a pain free tattoo with a lifetime guarantee!' continued the Language Monitor, eerily proud.

'How many citizens have been labelled already?'
'You are the first, Sir. We did not expect anyone to be

travelling back into Global City this time of night; especially as there is a curfew because of what is happening in the Sister Motherland. You have given us the opportunity to test it, thank you.'

'My pleasure. Everything is under control in the Sister Motherland,' said Norman, realising Area Blue no longer existed. 'You need not worry. What is your name?' asked Norman.

'Global Citizen Identity Number 201332,' he replied, robotically.

'Well I will be certain to tell Mr. Law that you have carried out the labelling procedure as per protocol,' continued Norman, not knowing if he had used the correct turn of phrase.

'Thank you, Sir,' replied the Language Monitor proudly, as they exited the booth.

The Language Monitor opened the car door for Linda and she thanked him and got in.

Norman started the engine and reversed the car. 'What were you doing in the booth?'

‘Nothing, the Language Monitor realised my position at the GSPC that’s all. He was apologising profusely, probably worried that he would be reprimanded. We are free to enter the city,’ he murmured, driving away.

‘What was the point of all that?’ asked Linda, ‘what’s the purpose of the machine?’

‘They are testing a new ID system,’ he replied, dismissively.

Norman decided that Linda did not need to know that she had been labelled by Mr. Law.

But, what neither of them knew was; in comparison to the label being inflicted on citizens in Area Blue who would not renounce their Mother Tongue, the planned GS labelling of all Global Citizens within Global City, the Motherland, the Sub Motherlands and those countries which had sworn allegiance to GSW, was a pain free work of art.

As Norman drove home to Global City to reunite with Georgia and her friends, Stephen replayed the CCTV footage of Norman and Linda receiving their GS label. He watched it over and over in glee, pleased with the Language Monitor’s performance. He would be sure to reward him.

‘Norman, Norman, Norman,’ he said pitifully, ‘will you ever learn?’

He sent a message to Claudia to instruct Phoebe Burnham to meet him in his office immediately. Phoebe’s encounter with Norman would tell him everything he wanted to know about Norman’s sudden appearance out of exile.

23

Norman had no idea how he was going to stop Stephen Law. He was in disbelief about the rapidity of the extension of the GSPC and GSW and the willingness with which nations were becoming globalised.

He recalled David's chillingly prophetic words all that time ago, that, "Convention is practically the same as law. GSW, that is Stephen Law, has a phenomenal vision to make GS, the one common language of the world. I believe it could work. I believe if these other countries adopt GS as an official language with a view to phasing out their various Mother Tongues, the GPC will be more than just a convention my friend."

Norman felt sickened by the reality of David's foresight. He pulled onto his Global City drive, grateful that he had been able to offer shelter to his visitors. These young people had risked everything to be in Global City but had no idea that the lifestyle they so desired came at such a high cost.

As Norman and Linda entered their home they heard laughter, warm laughter that lifted their spirits.

'Phoebe!' said Norman, surprised and pleased that Georgia had taken his advice to find her sister.

But, as Norman and Linda stood in their living room they felt like intruders. On their entrance the atmosphere changed. They thought these other youngsters for whom they, too, had risked everything, would be pleased to see them. But there was something obviously very wrong.

As Linda was about to speak, a luminous neon red light suddenly beamed through the window into the room.

'I'm sorry,' said Georgia, making her way towards the door.

Norman looked at Georgia perplexed by her apology.

'Time to go,' said Phoebe, determinedly.

'Go where?' asked Linda, 'where are you going? Georgia … ?'

'I'm sorry but this was the purpose of our journey. We have no intention of returning home. We want to be Global Citizens. Phoebe can protect us. If we renounce our Mother Tongue we will not be detained. We will be granted full citizenship.'

'If you do the same you will not be detained either,' said Phoebe.

'Detained? What do you mean?' asked Norman.

'By the Language Monitors,' confirmed Phoebe. 'If you come with me now Mr. Law will pardon you. You already bear the Global Standard label so this will be taken into consideration.'

'What label?' asked Linda, worriedly.

'On your palms. Just like mine.' As Phoebe turned her hands to show Linda, the neon light that engulfed the room turned to an ultra violet ray and illuminated the GS label.

Linda looked at her own palms and to her disbelief etched on her skin was the GS symbol. She scratched frantically at the marks trying to eradicate them, but no matter how hard she tore at the images they remained intact. She rushed agitatedly to the kitchen to attempt to wash the labels away but once out of the ultra violet light she could not see them. She scrubbed frantically but it was no use; the labels were indelible.

'I'm sorry,' said Norman, remorsefully to Linda. 'I had no idea that when we entered the booths we were automatically labelled as GS citizens.'

'It's futile to resist,' Phoebe admonished Norman; he was astonished that he had underestimated her loyalty to

Stephen Law. He'd assumed she would be only too delighted to return home on being reunited with Georgia. He didn't understand how he had read the situation so wrongly.

Norman and Linda watched helplessly as Georgia and her friends willingly marched to the vehicle to be transported to GSW HQ to swear allegiance to Global Standard and become Global Citizens.

Stephen Law watched the live stream of Norman and Linda's arrest for harbouring illegal citizens. Now, their remaining options were, renounce their Mother Tongue and live freely in Global City or be labelled in the same manner as their friends in Sister Motherland.

24

Stephen's instruction, 'Prepare to advance in the name of Global Standard,' assaulted Rod's conscience. He looked at his empty suitcase and decided he would abandon his post. He would flee Area Blue under the cover of darkness. He was overwhelmed with empathy for its Mother Tongue citizens. He guiltily longed to confess the real reason why he was there. But the directive by the region's Prime Minister had been issued and it was too late to stop Stephen Law marching into Area Blue and claiming it as a Global Standard region.

Rod had observed the Education Minister over the last few months and deduced that he was opposed to GSW and everything for which Global Standard and Stephen Law stood. But, like Rod, he did not have the courage to protest.

Strangely, Rod felt at ease about his decision. After all, how could the Language Monitors carry out their duties without their Language Warrior to give them instructions? He would leave immediately without giving any orders concerning Area Blue which would delay their departure from Global City. Rod reasoned that by the time Stephen realised the Language Monitors hadn't deployed, he would be long gone. Consequently, if Stephen then gave the order on Rod's behalf, it would take the Language Monitors at least three hours to make the journey from Global City. Dusk had already set, so Rod decided he would wait a while longer then depart covertly. 'But what about Angelina? I need to get word to her, to tell her to get out of Global City, to come home. I need to tell her … ,' he repeated, over and over, panicking.

He decided he would drive to the airport and wait on a flight; to where he didn't know but the further away the better. He would have to jettison his Global Passport, Identity, car, mini pc and all other items that belonged to Stephen Law's administration. As far as Rod was aware Stephen did not know where he came from so Rod concluded it would be easy to escape undetected. However, unknown to Rod, the mini pc that Stephen had confiscated the day he'd forced him to renounce his Mother Tongue, coupled with his acquaintance with Rod's sister, Angelina, provided Stephen with Rod's complete history.

'How will I explain myself to my mother?' he worried, anxiously. 'Does she even need to know my decision?' he considered, looking at his own country's passport. 'As long as I do not have to live my life any longer under the tyranny of Mr. Law or my parent's expectations, I can go wherever I want in the world,' thought Rod, feeling momentarily liberated.

He dialled Angelina's number which promptly played her answer phone message. He tried it once more praying she would reply but again the immediate response was the pre-recording.

'Who else can I trust?' he pondered. 'Joan, I can trust Joan. Surely she will agree that this has gone above and beyond GSW's original remit. She will see reason.' He dialled Joan's mini pc but the line rang out; he was unaware that she had left Global City.

'Who else is there that can stop this tyranny?' he questioned panic stricken, scrolling through his contacts. 'I must alert the Education Minister to what is about to happen. I must tell him that the Prime Minister has sworn allegiance to GSW and that he should flee. Maybe his staff will go with him? We could leave together. Yes, that's a good idea. We could leave together, right now.' As Rod frantically thought about his next move, he could hear a faint, uniform commotion in the distance that sounded like hundreds of marching feet. As he puzzled why the noise seemed familiar, it got closer, then closer still. Feeling very unnerved and sensing that the commotion had something to do with Stephen, he looked out of his window to see a host of Language Monitors parading up the street. The pyramid structure of the marching silhouettes that Stephen had showcased in his office, now made complete sense. The flag, neon red ties and lapels presented ghost-like in the night, by making the observer believe that these objects were floating and not attached to their host.

As the crescendo intensified, citizens came out of their homes to see what was happening. Those already outside were ordered to the pavements by the Language Monitors, where they watched the procession in trepidation and confusion.

'Stephen must have assumed the world leaders would vote in favour of Global Standard. He must have deployed these troops hours ago in readiness for the takeover,' thought Rod, floored by Stephen's audacity and his own naivety.

Rod's mini pc started to vibrate indicating that Stephen was trying to contact him. Rod looked at the device knowing that Stephen would expect him to answer forthwith. He momentarily ignored the insistent buzzing, reached under the bed for his suitcase and frantically grabbed his clothes from the wardrobe and chest of drawers. He threw them into his suitcase, zipped it and grabbed his coat knowing that his wallet, keys and passport were in his pocket.

The mini pc didn't relent and the longer Rod ignored it, the more frantically it buzzed, the noise becoming louder and louder.

Rod hastily grabbed hold of the door handle but as he pushed down to open the door, a red neon light engulfed the whole room. Rod turned to see what the intrusion was and had to cover his eyes from the glare. As Rod stood, nearly blinded by the light, the red glare calmed down enabling him to focus. But what he witnessed stirred disbelief.

'Going somewhere?' enquired Stephen Law. Rod dropped his suitcase to the floor.

'How… ,' he mumbled, 'how is this possible? How are you here?'

'Technology is a wonderful thing Rod. While you've been negating your duty as my Language Warrior, I and the technical team at GSW have pioneered this lifelike visual communication.'

Rod stood aghast, faced with a holographic image of Stephen in his room. It was so lifelike he had to remind himself that Stephen wasn't there. In fact, he still had time to run. A hologram couldn't chase after him, could it?

'Did I not tell you "prepare to advance in the name of Global Standard"; now go and salute your Language Monitors,' commanded Stephen, as a Language Monitor appeared in his doorway. Rod was flabbergasted as he realised his opportunity to leave had passed him by; it seemed that Stephen Law was literally ubiquitous and omnipresent.

'Collect the Education Minister and his staff and tell them to wait in the Parliamentary building for my next orders,' commanded Stephen.

Perplexed, Rod picked up his mini pc and trooped robotically out of his room to the Education Minister's office not questioning whether he and his staff would be there, even though it was late. As Rod opened the Minister's door, they all looked anxiously at him, wondering what was going on.

'Come with me,' he told them. 'Why?'

'You'll find out very soon,' replied Rod routinely, as they entered the street.

'What is this?' inquired the Education Minister, as hundreds of Language Monitors marched towards the government building.

'Follow me,' Rod repeated, 'you are expected in Parliament.'

'But why?'

Rod did not answer but instructed his Language Monitors to accompany the Education Minister and his staff. They formed a pyramid of obedience around him lodging him in the centre. He walked, trying to keep up with their quick march, feeling like a steered piece of cattle about to be trampled if he didn't obey. They reached the Parliamentary Building where, to the Minister's surprise, the Prime Minister was already waiting. Rod pondered how had he returned so quickly from Stephen's speech at the Hallowed Building? If the Minister is here then why isn't Stephen Law present in person, he wondered further.

Someone in the crowd recognised one of the Education Minister's staff and asked her, 'What is going on? Who are these people in uniform?' But the staff member truly did not know. All she knew was that the Education Minister had, clandestinely, been trying to halt a new language law that had the power to replace their Mother Tongue with Global Standard. All she knew was that the Education Minister had delayed this law from taking root; yet, now it seemed his efforts had been in vain.

'What's going on inside the Parliament Building?' the person demanded to know, causing others in the crowd to ask the same question.

'You. Yes, you, in that weird looking uniform. Is this some kind of joke? You. I'm talking to you,' shouted the annoyed citizen at a Language Monitor, trying to evoke a response.

'We need to get inside the building,' someone else bellowed.

'Follow me, I'll get answers,' yet another roared, determinedly. 'Let me pass,' he said threateningly to one of the Language Monitors in Mother Tongue. 'Let me pass, I won't tell you again.' The Language Monitors had been trained to ignore any inciting behaviour. They were well versed in anti-riot tactics. Mr. Law had warned them this would happen in regions where its citizens did not agree with the new Global Standard legislation.

As the crowd got rowdier and people prepared to storm the Parliament building, a luminous, neon red light shone into the night sky, dazzling the people into submission.

'Look,' said a bystander, 'there, in the sky,' she continued, pointing.

One by one, the people moved their attention from the edifice itself to the light that was beaming the "One Language, One Version, One Vision" motto into the dark night. The crowd quietened as they puzzled what this meant. Then, the familiar voice of the Prime Minister echoed into the darkness, almost as if emerging from the neon sign in approval of what was happening.

'Please, please, quiet. I have some exciting news,' he began in Global Standard. The crowd looked on in disbelief as their Prime Minister was not speaking to them in their Mother Tongue. They hushed their voices ready for an explanation. Despite Global being an official language, the Prime Minister was renowned for upholding their ancestral Mother Tongue. It was the recognised vernacular in the region and had been protected until now, allowing people the freedom to converse in it without fear of reprimand.

The Prime Minister began. 'The world is changing at a rapid rate. Our country is a precursor of this change. Our country is respected and revered as a historic nation that has never been afraid to embrace the future. So what does this future look like? It is a future of prosperity, status and empowerment for every citizen with no one being left behind. But, for us to truly benefit from this we need to be united. We need to think as one, communicate as one and be as one people with a common language. This is the future for our country and for the rest of the world. Global is on the rise and it has been chosen as the standard to which all other countries should aspire.

Global has been upgraded to Global Standard. It is already paving the way in the Motherland and many countries which have officially accepted it as THE recognised language of their nation. We must ensure that we champion this new law and acknowledge that Global Standard is the one uniform language of the whole Motherland: from our small piece of land to Global City. So, from this time forth, I am publicly announcing that we, citizens of the Sister Motherland will no longer speak any other language than Global Standard. We will no longer be devolved from other regions or Global City. We will be proud to be classified as a Motherland region. Mother Tongue will no longer be an accepted form of communication; spoken or written. Mother Tongue will form no part of our education or … .

Some Area Blue inhabitants looked on in shocked dismay as their Prime Minister simply dismissed their ancient language in the most matter-of-fact tone. Without any warning he just glibly proclaimed that their centuries old culture did not matter and would be eradicated with immediate effect. They were confused why he was referring to their homeland by a name which they did not recognise.

'It's happening again,' said an elderly Mother Tongue citizen, 'just like years ago when Global marched in and marginalised our rights to speak our own language.' The old man's son looked at his frail father, propped up by his walking stick. He, like so many of his generation, was familiar with the diabolical consequences of imposing Global on their country and he did not want it to recur.

'Dad, go home and let me deal with this. You're too frail to be in this crowd. Please go home,' he urged him. His father hugged him and left.

'We have been here once before,' the son cried out in Mother Tongue as he watched his father hobble away. 'History tells us that when the language oppressors tried to take away our culture, heritage and freedom, that our determination to maintain our identity won the battle and Global did not then, and will not now, overtake our way of life.'

As his voice projected objections into the night air, Mother Tongue supporters gathered around him to encourage him in his fervour. As his words competed with the Prime Minister's, some Area Blue citizens began to filter towards the Parliament's entrance, enticed by the promises that swearing allegiance to Global Standard would bring. As a pocket of Mother Tongue inhabitants looked on in distress that their fellow countrymen could be so easily coerced, a truck pulled up alongside them and one by one these insurgents were steered like cattle into the back of the vehicle by Language Monitors. These particular Language Monitors are a different breed of law enforcement that Stephen Law kept secret from Rod. These will eliminate from society any citizen opposed to Global Standard. Objectors will be transported to a place that Stephen has prepared for all language traitors. This is one of the consequences of which he spoke.

As the old man was hobbling down the street to the safety of his home, the truck hurtled past him, causing him to lose grip of his walking stick. As he bent to pick it up, he didn't notice that his son and many others of his friends' beloved children were crammed into the truck, as a punishment for daring to speak out against the new language law. As the days passed, people were missing husbands, wives, sons, daughters, cousins, aunts, uncles and friends. For some, who would not renounce their Mother Tongue they would join their loved ones. But for others, who were persuaded to swear allegiance to GS, they were unaware that they would be extradited from their family. Mother Tongue and Global Citizens DO NOT co-exist in society.

25

The Language Monitor pyramids on the right and left halted suddenly. The pyramid containing the Education Minister delivered him securely in the building.

'Stand down,' commanded Rod.

As they dispersed, the Education Minister stood alone, dazed by the events of the last few minutes. The Prime Minister extended his hand, directing him into a side room as he began to unfold the next stage in the proceedings.

The Language Monitors guarded the entrance to the hall, where the first Mother Tongue Renouncing Ceremony was about to take place. Rod knew his opportunity to flee had gone. He was trapped with nowhere to run. His earpiece vibrated, alerting him to an incoming communication from Stephen.

'Rod, you are obviously unaware that Joan Marsh has deserted her post at GSW. And as for your sister, I have no idea of her whereabouts. Were you trying to contact them for any reason? I cannot remember informing you that your covert operation had ended. Or did you misdial?' demanded Stephen, sarcastically.

Rod did not respond.

'A misdial. I assumed so. In a few minutes, the Education and Prime Ministers will emerge and this is what is going to happen. You will carry out the first ever Mother Tongue Renouncing Ceremony, just as rehearsed.'

Rod felt nauseous. He wanted no part of this. This was tyrannical. This was the beginning of a dictatorship. This was not right.

'I'm presuming you can remember the order of proceedings?'

'Yes, Sir,' responded Rod, feeling so disappointed in himself.

'Very good, let us begin. Place your mini pc on the table in the middle of the hall and I will make the presentation.'

'But how? You are not here?' quizzed Rod.

'Rod, Rod, Rod. Why do you still doubt?' sniggered Stephen.

Rod placed his mini pc as instructed by Stephen. The Prime Minister and the Education Minister appeared from the ante chamber and stood a few feet away, facing the table. The Language Monitors filled the room wanting to witness this historic moment.

The room was quiet, as they waited, eyes fixed on Rod. But Rod knew that he wasn't to speak yet, Stephen was first.

'Is he here after all?' Rod wondered, as he waited for the activities to commence.

Then, a shining light emerged from Rod's mini pc; the same red light that he had just experienced in his hotel room. It was so bright that everyone had to shield their eyes. Rod was the only one who knew what was coming next. When the light faded the life-size hologram of Stephen Law was projected into the atrium. But this was something else. This was obviously the deluxe version. Stephen was as large as life and seemed as real as anyone standing in the lobby.

He began to speak to the crowd. 'It is an honour for me to be with you today and address you as my official Language Monitors. I am proud to witness your loyalty to Global Standard and it is my privilege to share with you the first Mother Tongue Renouncing Ceremony.'

Rod couldn't believe the rapturous applause that these three short comments evoked from the Monitors.

Stephen continued, 'In a moment, Rod Jones, Head of Operations at GSW will begin the inauguration ceremony. This is a historic moment for GSW, the GSPC and Global Standard which has been made possible due to your fidelity to the "One Language, One Version, One Vision" edification that will truly make the world a better place. Powerful thinking inspires a brave new world begins here and now,' finished Stephen, to even more enthusiastic plaudits.

'Mr. Jones are you ready to begin?' asked Stephen, as if giving him a choice.

'Yes, Sir,' Rod replied.

'Then let the event commence,' announced Stephen.

As the Prime Minister and Education Minister stood facing Rod, he noticed that the latter was perspiring profusely and his complexion had turned a bright shade of scarlet.

'Prime Minister, you will be first,' confirmed Rod.

The Prime Minister stood to attention, his hands statue-like by his side. He looked at Stephen in awe of his accomplishments. His confidence, his zeal for something in which he believed, his private jet that had transported him back to Area Blue expediently to ensure this ceremony could proceed without delay. He felt honoured to be publicly stating his devotion to the GSW vision.

'Repeat after me,' Rod began. 'I, Prime Minister of the Sister Motherland swear allegiance to Stephen Law, GSW and the GSPC. I publicly declare that I support the One Language, One Version, One Vision system of Global Standard. I vow to uphold Global Standard and renounce this region's Mother Tongue. I hereby declare that from today, Global Standard will be the official language of this district and it will therefore be against the law to communicate or conduct any proceedings in Mother Tongue. I revoke our right to be a devolved government and agree to the new legislature that will join this region to Motherland and its governance by the GSW administration.' The Prime Minister repeated seamlessly, the words that sealed his allegiance to Stephen Law, GSW and Global Standard.

'I hereby officially declare you as Prime Minister of the Sister Motherland,' congratulated Stephen, as cheers and applause filled the atrium.

'Education Minister repeat after me,' Rod instructed, noticing that his bright red complexion was now ashen grey.

'I, Education Minister, swear allegiance … ,' Rod instigated. He waited for the reiteration but there was silence as the Language Monitors and Stephen Law looked on.

'I, Education Minister … ,' Rod started again. Yet, still, no response was forthcoming.

Then, the Education Minister, wiped his forehead, cleared his throat and began, 'I, Education Minister swear allegiance to … swear allegiance to … I Education Minister swear allegiance to my ancestral Mother Tongue and I will fight to protect its right to be spoken in this country with my dying breath. I do not pledge loyalty to Stephen Law, this holographic hallucination who is just a mere man, as am I. I declare allegiance to God and his mighty power that gave us languages as he purposed at Babel. I … ,' he continued in his Mother Tongue as the Language Monitors dragged him out of the room.

'Well, it would seem we have our first official language traitor. We will not allow this to hinder the spread of Global Standard. We will unite. We will show the world the consequences for such an act. Please bring the miscreant back so I can show my supporters the fate of anyone who does not renounce their Mother Tongue in favour of Global Standard,' ordered Stephen.

Rod nodded a command to the monitors who returned the minister.

'I'm sorry you feel this way about Global Standard,' boomed the holographic Stephen, whose apparition was now towering above the Minister.

'But don't worry, because I have already prepared a place for language traitors who dare to oppose my vision of taking Global Standard to the ends of the earth.'

Rod looked on, his stomach sinking fast, wondering what was the consequence Stephen hadn't yet divulged. They had rehearsed the ceremony but no one had defected. The flag bearer, who headed up the pyramid, passed the flag to Rod and produced what looked like an ink stamp from his belt pouch. As the crowd looked on, the flag bearer instructed the minister to place his right hand on the table.

'I will do no such thing,' protested the minister.

The monitors grabbed hold of him, pinned his hand to the table and spread his fingers placing a vice over his hand to keep his digits apart.

Then the flag bearer hoisted up the stamp and suddenly lowered it in one quick action onto the back of the minister's right hand causing him to cry out in anguish. The Language Monitor pressed on the newly labelled imprint with a heated compress to ensure the ink dried quickly and did not smudge. He then removed the contraption that had been separating the minister's fingers. Rod looked on in disgust at the LS label which stood for Language Suppressor, unable to take in what he had just witnessed. As Rod stood, holding the GSW flag, seemingly in approval of what the minister had just endured, he felt a shame that shattered him to the core as abruptly as the stamp had infiltrated the minister's senses.

As Stephen watched the Education Minister receive his label, his mind replayed his objection over and over. "I declare allegiance to God and his mighty power that gave us languages as he purposed at Babel." God, Babel, mighty power; these key words infiltrated his senses. Stephen looked at Rod and recalled Rod's Mother Tongue name, Nimrod Nazareth. He recalled how he had been lenient with Rod when he had found out that he was a language traitor because of his own sentimental attachment to the story of Nimrod and The Tower of Babel from the Bible.

'Papa, I remember, I remember,' he thought suddenly as images of himself as a child with Apollos, his late grandfather, reading this story to him from his Mother Tongue Bible flooded his memory. As the labelling continued, Stephen saw nothing except the words Nimrod, God, mighty power, Babel, Pentecost and tongues of fire floating around the room but they were not in Global Standard. As his eyes surveyed these words he scrutinized them and tried to decode their meaning. As he looked at each word, he heard a familiar voice, the voice of someone he knew he had loved very much and who had loved him abundantly in return. But the voice wasn't speaking in Global Standard. The voice was speaking another dialect; the utterances made Stephen feel calm and content and deeply cherished.

As the caressing voice continued he heard another word that he instantly recognised but it wasn't just a word it was a name, it was his name, his childhood name.

'Nastan, Nastan, Nastan,' whispered the voice lovingly.

'Stephen, Stephen, Stephen,' another voice interrupted patronisingly. 'Do not be taken in by sentiment. Feelings are fleeting. Emotion is short lived.

Status and power live on forever. What do you want to be remembered for STEPHEN?' asked the brooding presence.

As the familiarity of the Invisible Stranger's demands overshadowed Stephen's memory of the time before Global City, the Mother Tongue words evaporated. Stephen composed himself, publicly congratulated Rod Jones on his success in the Sister Motherland and watched as the Education Minister was escorted out of the parliamentary building in the same fashion that he arrived. As Stephen bid the crowd farewell to a joyful ovation, he caught a glimpse of the hazy silhouette on his balcony. Stephen ended the call on his mini pc which removed his holographic self from the atrium. He looked to the balcony, but his father figure had departed leaving nothing but a cold chill in the air.

26

'Please tell me, I can keep a secret,' nagged Aphia, ironically realising how much truth there was in her statement. She had lost count of the number of untruths she was keeping from Grigor.

'All will be revealed at the meeting,' he replied, 'until then, I am sworn to silence, even from you.'

Aphia huffed, knowing that Grigor was an honourable man and if he had given his word to the Councillors, she would have to wait for the official meeting to find out what The Language Town was all about and how it would help their region and country prosper.

When Grigor's secretary, Monica, had retired, he didn't know who would be worthy or capable of replacing her; she had been the Mayor's personal assistant for years, too many to remember. But Aphia saw this as the perfect opportunity to take on the role. She missed the business of her job at GSW.

'Are you qualified?' Grigor had asked her, not realising that his question was somewhat offensive. But of course he didn't mean anything by it. He assumed that Aphia hadn't had much cause for administrative duties while living in the mountain village. So yet again, Aphia told another lie.

'How difficult could it be? You can interview me and give me a typing test and see how I do,' she had told Grigor, trying to remain calm about how old-fashioned he could be when it came to business. 'That will keep the critics and sceptics happy. In fact, don't you interview me, get someone who is impartial. That way, if I pass, then I pass on my own merit and nobody can question your decision to hire me.'

'That's sounds more than fair,' agreed Grigor, admiring her confidence. Not realising that the role of PA to the Mayor was a doddle in comparison to the secretary of the free Global world.

'It's quite remarkable,' agreed the interviewing panel, 'Mrs. Saul certainly has all the necessary skills and attributes, Mr. Mayor. Where did she learn such skills? We thought she had been living in the mountain village.'

'My wife is a very tenacious lady,' said Grigor, wondering himself how she had scored so highly.

***

Aphia sat with pen and paper in hand, ready to scribe the minutes of the meeting. She had prepared the room, placing the agenda, a pen, paper and a glass of water for each attendee (the Mayors and Mayoress from the other regions). Grigor was hoping the meeting would secure their endorsement for the Language Town to proceed. In addition to this, he hoped they would emulate his ideas and plans for the Language Town in the other regions as was their NO GLOBAL policy.

Aphia glanced at Grigor, he was sat ready, waiting for the attendees. He looked anxious but would not look her way for reassurance. As far as Grigor was concerned she was there as his secretary and in front of her he would not show weakness. As the attendees started to arrive, Grigor greeted them and thanked them for coming. Then, in his capacity as Mayor, he stood up, asked for silence and hit his hammer onto the table as was tradition, to show the proceedings had commenced.

'Ladies and Gentlemen, if I could firstly ask you to spend the next few minutes looking over the agenda, then once you are familiar with the items we will begin,' he sat down, took a sip of water and adjusted his tie.

As the attendees took a few minutes to read the itinerary, Grigor's mind was suddenly taken back to the day Apollos had died in that very building. He recalled the disorder and dishonour of that day. He remembered how some of the town's own citizens had called for Mother Tongue to be replaced with Global. He remembered running frantically out of the museum and trying to find Dr. Mitrov. He thought crossly about his teenage friend, Nastan Popov and how Nastan had witnessed his grandfather die before his very eyes. Resentment and bitterness towards Nastan suddenly engulfed Grigor as he remembered how Nastan had dishonoured Apollos with his love for all things Global. Yet, he was equally grateful to him because if Nastan had become the leader of the Youth Movement all those years ago, instead of Grigor, Grigor's life would have taken a completely different path. He would not be here at this point in history still defending his country against language traitors such as Nastan Popov.

'Global killed Apollos,' he pondered, poignantly. 'The talk of Global replacing Mother Tongue was too much for him to bear,' he recalled, painfully. Grigor reminisced with thankfulness the dedication Apollos had shown to their language, culture and heritage. How he was still loved by the people of their town who, to this day, affectionately refer to him as Papa Popov. He visualised the memorial plaque on the statue that had been erected, in his memory:

"Apollos Popov, language upholder, patriarch and Chairman of the Minority Language Council. A deeply missed friend".

After Apollos' death, Grigor's father had been honoured to accept the Chairmanship in memory of their beloved Papa Popov. Grigor had assured his predecessor,

Jakov, many years ago, that he would ensure Global would never infiltrate their country; he had made a promise to uphold their language, no matter what. Now, all these years later, that promise would be further cemented with the establishment of the Language Town. And as for Nastan Popov, after sharing Grigor's home and family after his grandfather's death, once he realised that he had money to attend the International School, he left to become Global itself. Grigor remembered the parting gift he had covertly given to Nastan and wondered if it had devoured his conscience and life in the way that he'd intended – the day he'd left town was the last time they saw each other.

As the attendee's eyes left the pieces of paper on which the agenda was detailed and gazed at Grigor, he felt the need to say something in memory of Apollos.

'I would like to start the proceedings by jumping to the last item on the agenda, namely "any other business". While we are gathered here today in this delightful building, which is still the hub of our wonderful language, I would like us to take a minute to remember our beloved Apollos Popov. His statue sits outside this building so we will never forget the sacrifices he made for his town, country and language. He, along with Jakov, was a true language upholder and he spoke plainly concerning the demise of our Mother Tongue. The legacy left by Apollos and Jakov has ensured that our beloved and ancient language is protected by the Minority Languages World Association. Their fervour to keep Global out has allowed us to enjoy that protection to this day.'

As Aphia began scribing Grigor's heartfelt words her mind was suddenly drawn to Phoebe and something she had said concerning their hometown while they were in Global City. "Statue man," she recalled Phoebe saying.

"Statue man dropped dead because of the shock that someone from his own generation would stand against their language."

'Mrs. Saul,' she heard Grigor saying faintly. 'Mrs. Saul,' she heard him saying again, louder. Aphia realised that she had stopped scribing.

'Are you quite alright, dear?' asked the Mayoress, concerned by how ghostly white her complexion had become. She looked blankly at the Mayoress.

'Maybe someone could get Mrs. Saul a glass of water and we will continue in a moment,' she suggested, addressing Grigor.

'Water, yes, of course,' he replied briskly, leaving the room, wondering why Aphia had yet again turned a ghostly shade; it seemed to be happening all too often. It was really beginning to worry him.

The Mayoress continued addressing Aphia but her thoughts were not in the room. Her thoughts were at her apartment in Global City when Phoebe had insinuated that Aphia's grandmother had caused the death of Apollos Popov – Statue man.

'Here you go my dear,' said the Mayoress, handing Aphia the water. Aphia took a few sips and then passed it back to her, who in turn passed it back to Grigor.

'I'll leave it here for you,' said Grigor to his wife, trying to be understanding but also conscious that as Mayor and leader of the meeting he had to get back to business.

The Mayoress spoke again, 'Mr. Mayor, given that your clerk is obviously unwell maybe you should consider using this wonderful little device that will record your words. I am sure none of us will object.'

Grigor looked at the device with distain; not because he didn't approve of technology; the plans for the

Language Town would mean they would be heavily reliant on technology. But this was not the way business was conducted in a council meeting. The minutes were always scribed; it had been that way for ever.

'That's a wonderful idea,' agreed one of the Mayors, causing the others to approve.

Aphia collected her notebook and pen and rather shakily left the room.

'Maybe you should go straight to Doctor Mitrov,' said Grigor quietly in her ear. She nodded and left. Grigor pressed the record button on the Dictaphone and began the proceedings, disappointed that Aphia would have to wait a while longer to hear his plans for the Language Town.

Aphia did not go to see Doctor Mitrov, knowing that what was making her feel unwell, could not be made better by a medical examination.'

27

'We concur,' confirmed the Mayoress, speaking on behalf of the attendees after hearing Grigor's plans for the Language Town.

'This truly is an exciting time for our country. Your idea for our culture and language is visionary,' she said, shaking his hand.

'I agree,' confirmed another Mayor, 'I will be making a recommendation within my own municipality to ensure your plans are emulated.

'As will I,' confirmed yet another Mayor.

As they congratulated Grigor and left the museum, there was one other person that was eager to shake his hand.

'Son, I couldn't be prouder,' said his father emotionally. He hadn't been allowed into the meeting despite being the Chairman because of their family connection. 'You gained full support which is a true indication of the backing of the Mayors and Mayoress.'

'I couldn't agree more,' said a teary Monica, who was more than happy to step out of retirement for a few hours. When Grigor had pressed record on the machine and it would not work, he took it as a sign that he should uphold tradition. The attendees agreed and waited patiently for Monica to come and take Aphia's place.

As Grigor left the museum and walked past Apollos' statue, he felt a true sense of kinship. He felt honoured that people whom Apollos had held in such high esteem showed equal respect to his memory by supporting Grigor's plans for the Language Town, which meant that Mother Tongue would be even further protected from Global.

Grigor returned home and saw Aphia's notebook and pen on the kitchen table. He called out for her but she did not respond. He headed to the lake, knowing that she would be there. If she wasn't home she was always at the lake.

As Aphia sat, contemplating how and when she would tell Grigor the truth she felt a casting shadow hovering over her. She looked up but was unable to see the face of the eerie figure because the brightness of the sun was causing her vision to blur. She looked once more but the sun cast a haze over the silhouette making her feel uneasy. She knew logically that the only person it would be was Grigor. If she wasn't home, he always came to the lake to find her. So how was this faceless stranger causing her palms to sweat and her heart to palpitate?

'Aphia, Aphia,' she could hear someone call which was interjected by another voice calling 'Joan.' Feeling somewhat unnerved, she hesitantly rose to her feet. Relieved to see Grigor standing there, she blurted emotionally, 'I'm so sorry. I don't know what came over me. One minute I felt fine, then the next … .'

'It's okay. What did Doctor Mitrov say?'

'Doctor Mitrov … it's just a virus. Sometimes it can linger for weeks but he said it would clear up on its own,' fabricating another lie.

'That's good news. Just a virus.'

'I'm feeling much better. If you want, we can head home and I'll transcribe the recording.'

'It's already been taken care off. Monica came to the rescue. I think she was glad to feel needed. I was so glad not to use that machine.'

'Oh, okay, that's good,' said Aphia, feeling quite replaceable.

'But don't worry. She insisted it was a one off and she was far too busy to be available at such short notice again.'

'So tell me, did they vote in favour?'

'The vote? In favour of what?' said Grigor, spiritedly.

Aphia looked at him and just knew that they had all agreed with Grigor's plans for the Language Town.

'Now that it's official you have access to my report which will give you everything you want to know.'

Grigor was elated that at last, after months of waiting Aphia could now read the plans. Now that he had the go ahead, as far as Grigor was concerned, the Language Town could proceed without delay and Global would never cause tribulation in their country.

***

'Don't hover over my shoulder or I'll never finish reading,' said Aphia protesting.

'I'm sorry, I'm just so eager to hear what you think,' he replied enthusiastically.

'Why don't you cook the fish you caught this morning and then we can chat about your plans while we eat.'

'Excellent idea,' said Grigor, leaving her in peace to digest the information.

Aphia relaxed into her veranda chair and placed her shawl snuggly around her shoulders. She loved this time of day. The heat of the sun had gone, yet it was still warm enough to sit outside. She opened the binder which contained Grigor's proposal and began to read.

As Aphia finished reading she felt dismayed by the concept of the Language Town. Even though Grigor claimed to be concerned for the protection of their Mother Tongue by ensuring that Global was prohibited, it gave the impression that the plan was directed at one person.

Aphia wondered to whom Grigor was so opposed. The directive read as, "Dear whoever you are. If you think you are going to come into my town, into my country; if you think you can persuade people to relinquish their Mother Tongue for Global, then come, because I am ready and waiting."

The construct of The Language Town was made up of a new decree that would ensure Global would not be spoken in their country, by its citizens or tourists. In addition to this, it would reaffirm that it played no part in educational law or society. The International Schools in their country, where Global was taught as a first language had already closed, causing families and staff to leave and move to a place where they were free to teach, learn and speak Global.

Aphia couldn't understand why Grigor and the other leaders would be okay with an exodus of their people. Surely, this was just the beginning of people leaving for good if they had to live with such restrictions. And what about the Global speaking tourists who loved visiting their land for skiing and fishing? How would Grigor explain such prejudice to them? What was even stranger was that the proposal, if it had been in Global, could have been written by Stephen Law. The similarity in the writing style, the use of certain words when Aphia processed them into Global reminded her so much of Stephen Law's vision for Global Standard to the world.

'How much is the Language Town going to cost, Grigor?' asked Aphia commandingly, 'you haven't listed cost projections in your report.' Aphia knew that technology came at a high price. She had been surrounded by all types of equipment at Global City and had been privy to authorising invoices from suppliers. Aphia often wondered how Stephen had gained so much wealth to maintain his plans. How was their country going to sustain the Language Town?

'Surely the municipality doesn't have the kind of wealth that this technological innovation and up-keep would require,' she observed, astutely.

Grigor defensively replied, 'We have been prudent. The municipality has budgeted very carefully for the Language Town. It has been my vision and purpose for our town and country since I was a teenager, when I became the leader of the Minority Language Youth Movement. Maybe you were just a little too young to remember the start of the Youth Movement. The then Mayor, Jakov, my predecessor, do you remember him? Did you ever meet him on one of his visits to the mountain village? He visited there regularly; he loved the old generation language upholders that live on the mountain. Did your grandmother ever speak of him? I'm certain she would have known him well.'

He continued babbling at full speed, not wanting to directly answer Aphia's questions, 'It has been my vision and purpose to see our language protected in honour of Jakov and Apollos. I've had to ensure that Global has been kept out. It was only me; only I wanted to take on the responsibility. It should have been Nas … .' Grigor stopped suddenly.

'It should have been?' questioned Aphia.

'Never mind. The Language Town has been my vision and purpose for keeping Global out for as long as I can remember. I will not allow anyone to let Global overtake our town and country. I would die first.'

Aphia sniggered at Grigor's comments, 'You would die first. That's an extreme stance don't you think?'

Grigor looked sternly at Aphia. She was shocked by his demeanour, by his obsession with Global. She suddenly felt she'd returned to Global City and was in the GSW epicentre. But the only difference was that the person who was laying down a language law was not Stephen Law but Grigor; calm, safe, secure, Grigor.

'You're right. I was too young to remember. I would only have been about seven or eight years old. You could tell me.'

Grigor stared intently ahead in silence. Aphia waited, also in silence, observing Grigor's demeanour; he seemed deeply troubled. As Aphia was about to prompt him once again, he painstakingly began his recollection.

'We were best friends; inseparable. We knew each other's thoughts. We could finish each other's sentences. But it all ended when he replaced me with Global,' said Grigor, unforgivingly.

Aphia felt uncomfortable as she detected the loathing in his voice when he said the word, Global.

'He. Who's he?' she asked.

'Nastan Popov; Apollos Popov's grandson, it should have been him who upheld our language. He should have stepped up as the Youth Movement Leader. But Global had possessed him. It had become his obsession. He wanted to learn it, speak it and become it. He was in favour of Global replacing our Mother Tongue. He killed his own grandfather.'

'How?' she asked, alarmingly, recalling how Phoebe had implied that Aphia's grandmother had been responsible for "statue man's" death. But now it would seem that someone else was culpable.

'By not accepting the Mayor's "call to arms". By literally breaking Apollos' heart and not becoming the

Youth Movement Leader; and then, after he found out that Apollos had left him money, a lot of money, he deserted his heritage, turned his back on me and my family and went to live at the International School in the city to become Global.'

'Where is he now, this Nastan Popov?'

'Who knows? The Mayor, before he died, felt remorse and shame for letting Nastan leave. He thought he had not cared about him enough and had only cared about protecting Mother Tongue. He placed an advert in the Global Times Newspaper, publicly seeking him but he didn't respond.'

'But why did he place an advert in a Global newspaper?' enquired Aphia, perplexed that Jakov would have sought answers from a Global source.

'Because that was the only way he could think of to contact him. The Global Times translated the message into Global so Jakov didn't think he was being disloyal to Mother Tongue. He also went to the International School hoping he was still there but he had already moved on.'

'Why did Nastan's leaving play such an important role in protecting Mother Tongue?'

Grigor was stumped. He did not want to tell Aphia everything. He did not want her to know about Nastan's father and how he was the Language Ambassador for their country and was in support of Global replacing Mother Tongue. He did not want to tell her how he had surreptitiously placed the Global language version blueprint that Stephen Popov was planning to use to replace Mother Tongue with Global, in the boot of the taxi transporting Nastan to the International School. He did not want to admit to her that he had anonymously done this, hoping that Nastan's Global obsession would become his downfall. He did not want to tell it all … there was too much to tell.

'I don't know,' he said, covering his comments, 'at the time the Mayor seemed to think that letting Nastan move to the school to enable him to fulfil his dreams was the best thing for him. But as the Mayor got older and dementia set in, he was plagued with remorse over Nastan. He believed he had neglected Nastan's needs as a bereaved teenager. He felt shameful that he hadn't taken care of him. He thought he had let Apollos down by allowing Nastan to be a lonely, orphan who lived a meagre existence in the International School.'

Aphia was confused. 'Why would Nastan leaving town have any effect on the future of Mother Tongue?'

Grigor continued, 'No one has ever heard from or seen him since. I've been expecting him, I've anticipated his visit, but so far, there's been no sign of him – the language traitor.'

Aphia felt alarmed that, all these years later, Grigor still felt betrayed by his childhood friend. His reference to him as a language traitor surely should have ended a long time ago. She didn't understand why Grigor still felt so threatened by this Nastan Popov. Why had he been expecting him if no one knew of his whereabouts? He was just a boy when he left home. Surely the conditions in which he left were to be pitied.

'So statue man … .'

'Who?' asked Grigor, puzzled.

'Sorry, Apollos Popov died protecting our language from the generations who believed that it should be replaced with Global.'

'Yes. He died knowing that the majority in our town, including his own grandson, held no regard for their own language.'

'So you took on the responsibility. You became Nastan Popov.'

'I most certainly did not. I was prepared for him to be the frontrunner and I would be his second in command.

His grandfather was the Chairman of the Minority Languages Association and it was the natural order that Nastan should be the young Apollos. I did what he should have done; what was expected of him. It was his duty to take on the role but he didn't want it. He shunned it, he was just like his fath …,' said Grigor, stopping abruptly yet again, hoping Aphia hadn't processed his last remarks.

He continued, 'And then everyone in the museum started attacking the Mayor, not physically but verbally. The majority called for Global to replace Mother Tongue, saying it was the only way for us to prosper and if we did not embrace Global we would be left behind. This traitorous behaviour was too much for Apollos to endure and it killed him. Global killed him. I ran out of the museum to get Doctor Mitrov, but by the time I returned it was too late, Apollos had gone. I had missed his very last minutes on earth. Nastan was there, standing over him, gloating, glad because he could get on with his Global life.'

Aphia recalled the scene; Phoebe's exposition concerning her grandmother and how she had caused the Mayor's death placed Aphia's child-self, at the museum. She remembered a teenage boy, pleading with an old man, pleading with him not to go, not to die. Without doubt, this was the moment to which Grigor was referring. Another untruth rested heavily on Aphia. 'Should I tell Grigor the part my own grandmother played in that day?' she deliberated.

'I think you are wrong. I can recall that day,' she began, hoping her words would flow naturally into a confession of the truth. 'I can remember there were lots of angry voices and then everyone left the museum. I remember my grandmother holding my hand and I was dragging my heels because I didn't want to leave. I was so mesmerised by the old man. There was a boy pleading with him not to die, telling him how much he loved him. I remember looking back just as we were leaving the museum and the boy was holding the old man's face in his hands. The man, Apollos, he looked miraculous. He looked like he was just asleep. I can remember looking at my grandmother and not being scared about her dying because if that's what death looks like, then why be afraid?'

As Aphia told Grigor about her memory from that day, she further recalled her grandmother speaking up in favour of Global. She remembered how aghast some people had been and now realised why; someone of her grandmother's generation supporting such a radical notion would have caused division. She further recalled the same teenage boy, looking at her grandmother with wonderment as she declared that they should make Global available in all their schools, so that the next generation would be able to communicate with the outside world.

Aphia's thoughts were transfixed as she realised that the teenage boy who'd looked at her grandmother with such reverence was Nastan Popov. Yet, there was also something unnervingly familiar about her memory of him.

'You must be mistaken,' interjected Grigor, 'you just said you couldn't remember and now you can recall all that. You are just trying to make me feel better.'

'I promise Grigor, that is what has just come flooding into my memory,' said Aphia, sincerely, omitting that she had recently heard an account of that day, which no doubt had sparked her recall.

'Nastan hated his grandfather for not allowing him to speak Global. I doubt very much he was upset when he died. He certainly did a good job of disguising his feelings. He couldn't wait to leave to learn a language that his grandfather despised. The very language that took his life,' he retorted, not prepared to hear another explanation.

Yet, still, Aphia could not bring herself to offer an alternative account; she could not bring herself to offer her grandmother as the culprit for Apollos' death. She could not do it.

Aphia looked at the report once more and wondered if Grigor had written it specifically with the language traitor, Nastan Popov, in mind. But why would a teenager have so much power over Global replacing Mother Tongue? Aphia looked at Grigor; his face indicated that he was in pain, emotionally not physically. She wondered if his out of character demeanour was being caused by this teenage recollection.

Grigor's supposition about Nastan's proclivity for Global, coupled with his plans to keep Global out of their country bombarded her consciousness. There was a similarity about her present and past situation which momentarily haunted her. Then, Aphia's stomach churned as the memory of Nastan's face intertwined with Stephen Law's.

Grigor's derogatory comments about Nastan and the content of his report infused her whole being. Threads were forming in her mind linking Grigor to Nastan and Nastan to Stephen, despite her attempts to disassociate them:

"... if it had been in Global this report could have been written by Stephen Law and intended for the Motherlands. The fusion of the writing style, the concepts, the phraseology were a replica of Stephen Law's vision for Global Standard to the world. Only this was Grigor's plan for eradicating Global."

Aphia plunged even deeper into an analysis of Stephen as she recalled the times that his Global, perfect as it was, occasionally stopped mid-sentence, as if he was making sure his words were perfectly formed before he carried on speaking. She remembered how Stephen's off-guard accent had once reminded her of how her grandmother, Aphia Joan, had sounded when she'd tried to learn Global.

Grigor's comments echoed around her mind. "No one has ever heard from or seen Nastan since …, to become

Global …, Global had possessed him …, it had become his obsession …, he wanted to become it … ."

'NO,' screamed Aphia internally. 'NO, I won't believe or accept it; it's just not possible … NO!' she wretched convulsively as she tried to reject every notion that Nastan Popov and Stephen Law were one and the same.

Aphia's sudden realisation of who she worked for and from where his obsession stemmed flooded her very being. She had been working alongside Grigor's nemesis and supporting the RISE of Global Standard. Yet now, the world she inhabited and the life she had chosen was in direct conflict to Stephen Law. 'How can this be? How has my life taken this direction?' she questioned, bewildered.

Aphia suddenly realised that Grigor's candour was justified as she concluded that it was only a matter of time before Stephen marched into Area Orange and declared it a Global region. However, she had no idea how far Stephen's vision had advanced since she'd left Global City. Grigor's guardedness proved well deserved.

Aphia observed Grigor who winced with discomfort. If her conclusion was correct, the secrets he was keeping from her concerning Nastan Popov were minor in comparison to hers. Once again she was flabbergasted that she always seemed to have the upper hand when it came to secrets and lies. She realised that keeping Stephen Law out of Area Orange was as much to her advantage as to Grigor's, their families and their country. She sensed she was running out of time.

28

Aphia was woken by the noise of yet another lorry containing supplies for the construction of the new Language Town. There was a positive atmosphere generally amongst the people because these activities were providing much needed work. Local tradesmen were employed and, as Mayor, Grigor was extremely proud of the skilled workers they had in their town.

Aphia looked out of her bedroom window and spotted Grigor in the near distance wearing a white construction hat and a bright orange high visibility jacket. The orange hue of his clothing brought Stephen Law's GSW world map to her mind which coded countries by colour. She recalled her conversation with Phoebe which had flummoxed Joan when she discovered they were from the same country.

"We are coded orange on the GSW map," Phoebe had stated.

But Aphia was roused out of her reverie by the unwelcome recollection that she had been unable to discuss the Language Town with Grigor any further, as he had been quite dismissive of her concerns and questions ...

"Grigor, you cannot stop people speaking Global and disguise your prejudice as a wonderful Language Town holiday experience," she had voiced, concerned.

"The NO Global policy is not a new idea, Aphia. This Global restriction has been in place since I became Mayor."

Grigor had continued irately, "I have tolerated Global speaking tourists believing they are elite and superior, but I cannot and will not any longer. If Global speakers want access to our town and country they will leave Global behind at the checkpoint. If they are not prepared to obey the rules, they will not be able to experience our language town."

"But you are not opposed to other languages being spoken publicly by tourists, just Global?"

"Exactly, just Global. But you are also missing the point. When tourists enter The Language Town they won't want to speak any other language except ours. This is why they are coming here, to learn Mother Tongue."

"So what if tourists still want to come and they follow the language rules, only conversing in Global in the privacy of their accommodation? What will happen to them if they're overheard? Will they be forcibly removed?"

Grigor had laughed, "Now whose being extreme? But that is an excellent point! No Global should indeed be NO GLOBAL; publicly and privately whilst participating in the Language Town experience."

"So will there be any publicity in Global to promote the Language Town? Even Jakov realised that Global played its part in marketing and administration?" queried Aphia, recalling, yet again, Phoebe's comments.

"There's no need. We will attract other language users. We do not need or want Global speakers any longer. The Language Town will ensure that we generate enough revenue to remain an independent state without appealing to Global speaking tourists."

Aphia had been dumbfounded. She felt as if she'd left one dictatorship for another. The only difference was that Grigor was disguising his language law as a holiday experience where visitors could push their linguistic boundaries by embracing a new language and a new experience – the first of its kind in the world! That was the advertising campaign running in many languages, except Global, of course.

"What will happen, Grigor, when the Global tourists who have been visiting here for years arrive? How are you going to explain your hatred of Global to them? Why would they possibly want to continue holidaying here?"

"They won't and that's the point."

Aphia had been shocked by his response. It had become increasingly apparent that Grigor had one intended goal which was to eradicate every ounce of Global from their country. Aphia was concerned that Grigor, like Stephen Law, had his own obsession which he was mistaking for the greater good of their town and country. Aphia felt helpless as she sat and watched the world that she had only just rediscovered, spiralling out of control. All the lies Aphia had told to protect her identity seemed of little significance considering what was happening. She was astonished that her new life had startling similarities to her old in Global City. The comparisons were alarming. Grigor, like Stephen, was trying to hinder the use of language. Stephen's vision was to make Global Standard the one common language of the world and Grigor's was to eradicate all traces of Global in their town and country.

Of course, since she had made the connection between Grigor and Stephen it made complete sense that they would have kindred, yet opposing, visions - albeit stirred by different motives. Aphia felt suddenly overwhelmed; she thought this was her safe haven, yet chaos was emerging from everywhere. She so wanted a normal life, something she thought she had found with Grigor. She looked at him despairingly and decided that whilst he was preoccupied she would take a trip to her grandparents' grave. She now felt ready to face the mountain village.

29

Grigor re-read his report pleased with how the plans for the town were proceeding. The first phase was to build a gated checkpoint through which all tourists entering the town would have to pass. This guaranteed that all non-Mother Tongue devices were handed into the Language Guards. A sign had been constructed which reinforced that the Language Town was a strictly NO GLOBAL zone for the tourists.

Grigor thought back to Aphia's comments about how people should be allowed to speak their own language wherever they were in the world. He felt disappointed and saddened that she did not understand what he was trying to achieve. That his actions would safeguard their town and country from being globalised. His decision as Mayor to banish Global may have seemed harsh, but he did not want their culture smothered by it nor their language to return to extinct status like so many other vernaculars across the planet. These countries had naively embraced Global as their official language, forsaking their Mother Tongue. He had made a promise to Jakov to be the language upholder and he would not fall short. He would do whatever was necessary to ensure the next generation revered their language. He would ensure they didn't sell out to Global, as Nastan's father had done all those years ago. If Stephen Popov's plans had come to fruition, their language would already be obsolete.

The construction plans for the Language Town were twofold in order to accommodate the influx of anticipated tourists. They included revamping existing guesthouses and Grigor's quick fix, namely building low cost, plasterboard bungalows for those who wished to self-cater. The bulk of the budget was reserved for the technology that would be paramount to the success and experience of the Language Town.

Every municipality within the country was bordered by a green belt which each Mayor agreed was essential for the safeguarding of the country's fauna and flora. The Mayors had signed a protection policy which meant that the natural habitat would remain unspoilt and would never be used to accommodate residential or industrial buildings. Grigor's country took great pride in the many indigenous mammals found there and that their green belt was a haven for endangered species.

For as long as Grigor could remember, the road that linked the neighbouring hamlet to their town was a dirt track. Over the years, as people had acquired cars and motorbikes, the road had widened naturally but it looked very unkempt. This clearly needed rectifying. Grigor wanted to make certain that all paying guests were uplifted by the Language Town experience, which, as far as he was concerned, began as they approached the town. At the end of this new road would be the gated entrance which would also serve as the checkpoint for the surrendering of all devices to the Language Guards. The holiday makers would sign a declaration that they were willing to relinquish their gadgets of their own free will on condition that they would be returned on departure. All documentation had been translated into the newcomer's language upon payment for the holiday. All nationalities were welcome, except, of course, Global speakers.

To Grigor's delight, several people had shown great pleasure at being able to holiday in a country where they would not be subjected to Global but he was grieved when one holiday maker referred to it as a *killer language* as it brought back painful memories of Apollos Popov. However, Grigor was unsure what that same tourist had meant by Global Standard, assuming that it was an error in translation from her language to his. Grigor loved that people wrote to him in his own language and that they were already learning his country's Mother Tongue in preparation for their holiday experience. But this one letter stood out to him as he kept recalling the phrase Global Standard.

The pinnacle to the whole Language Town experience is Grigor's symbol invention. A simple, yet highly effective means of non-Mother Tongue speakers being able to communicate with the townsfolk during their stay, whilst affording them the opportunity to acquire new language skills. On arrival to the Language Town each holiday maker is given a touch-screen device pre-programmed with hundreds of pictures and phrases. When the guest selects a picture, the Mother Tongue word is spoken allowing them to repeat the word, hence affording them the linguistic experience of speaking another language. There are phrases upon phrases available to enable the holiday maker to: order a meal, hire a bike, purchase groceries; all in Mother Tongue. Each holiday maker is assigned a Language Host whose job is to accompany them during their stay and assist with learning and communicating in Mother Tongue. The Language Hosts wear the countries' national dress which makes the whole experience even more authentic. Each evening there is entertainment in the town square where different aspects of culture can be experienced. The square is overtaken by festivities and traditional food dishes which are included within the cost of the holiday. If holiday makers wish to participate in other activities, such as fishing, skiing or just simply exploring the area accompanied by the guide, they pay an additional price for their Language Host to accompany them.

Grigor reached the penultimate page of his report. His plans filled him with joy. The costs, which Aphia had quizzed him about, were detailed on the final page. He separated that page from the others and placed it securely, out of sight, in the bottom draw of his filing cabinet, deciding that he would not look at it again until the Language Town was finished and ready to accommodate its first guests.

30

As the sun rises over the newly globalised Sister Motherland, the "One Language, One Version, One Vision" centre piece, which is the crowning glory of the Parliamentary Epicentre, illuminates more consistently than the sun, as it never dims day or night. The neon sign which reinforces the status of Global Standard to Sister Motherland Citizens', is visible from all vantage points.

Despite resistance to the new language law by a minority, this region now shares the Motherland's one common language – Global Standard. As envisioned by Stephen Law, the former Area Blue, no longer has its ancestral language identity and ALL citizens who oppose the new language decree are labelled.

As for those who willingly renounce their Mother Tongue, they believe wholeheartedly in the vision and purpose of GSW and the GSPC. They, like all Global Citizens, are truly invigorated by the morning colour they now associate with dawn. These citizens feel no guilt concerning the language traitors who will be punished for their treachery. Neither do they feel remorse for forsaking their family and friends in the name of Global Standard. The ideology and language shared between Global Citizens forms a stronger bond than any familial ties or friendships. Heritage seems unimportant in light of what one common language for the whole world will make possible; united like-minded citizens with true desire and commitment to GSW. They are proud to belong to the One Language, One Version, One Vision realm, even to ensuring that all Mother Tongue literature is burnt in the towers erected for this specific purpose.

For Global Citizens, in all GSW regions, the concrete towers are a symbol of the commitment and belief that they have in Stephen Law. They do not want language traitors in their midst. They pay little attention when the Global Standard trucks transport the defectors to a secret location where they are held until they renounce their Mother Tongue and become true Global Citizens, or endure the consequences.

***

As Stephen watched from GSW Headquarters the live stream from the Sister Motherland of the last tower being erected, he felt elated. He glanced at the TV monitors on his office wall that showed activity within other Globalised regions and the already established GSW zones. He was amused that Global Citizens were quite naturally going about their day, whilst Language Monitors kept the flames alive by destroying the evidence that their Mother Tongue ever existed.

As Stephen observed the flames dancing with exuberance, he recalled a time when he was a teenager. He remembered his grandfather, Apollos and how he had thrown a leaflet concerning Global into the fire and watched it burn. This recollection rekindled the feeling of anger that had engulfed him all those years ago as the word Global turned to ash before his very eyes.

He smiled with glee as the history of yet another language was burnt to a cinder. He studied the interactive GSW world map that decorated one side of his office wall. He looked at the hue that symbolised the Sister Motherland recalling that it should have been orange as was his own country. He had chosen this area as the

Guinea pig blueprint for globalisation and was now ready to emulate his Global Standard plan in his hometown. He puzzled why Norman had gone against his instructions and coded it blue? He concluded that the hue of the region no longer mattered because it was unrecognisable as a Mother Tongue province. Sister Motherland had earned its place as a bonified Global Standard region.

He scrolled to the select colour icon on the control panel of his p.c. and placed his right index finger on the blue hue, swiping simultaneously to the right. Then, with the same digit, he selected black which instantly replaced the azure label. He recalled the day, years before, when he had placed his father's original map over his GSW map and how the blue and orange colours fused into the deepest black – the colour that all citizens of the world will come to associate with Global Standard. It brought to mind his decision that Area Blue would be his test case, his pilot scheme, from which he would conquer all other Mother Tongue areas.

So, with the language law fully operational in the Motherlands, Sister Motherland and those countries that had already adopted GS, he was closer than ever to the next phase of fulfilling his father's original dream; the renunciation of Mother Tongue in favour of Global Standard in Area Orange, his home town.

'Close your eyes until I tell you to open them,' said Grigor, beaming.

'Okay, but you know I don't like surprises. Can't I just see it tomorrow the same as everyone else. It doesn't seem fair that I get a sneak preview.'

'That's the privilege of being married to the Mayor,' he said, unashamedly.

'You'll have to walk a little because I need you to see the whole effect, but, don't worry, I'll guide you.'

Aphia held Grigor's hand and she hesitantly put one foot in front of the other, wondering why she wasn't stumbling on the unkempt road that was full of potholes. 'I don't understand why the road seems so smooth?

Where are the potholes? Why aren't I wobbling as I usually do when I walk this dirt track?' Aphia queried.

'You'll see. Just walk for a few more feet.' Aphia carried on, guided by Grigor.

'Okay, you can stop. But don't open your eyes until I say.'

'Okay,' she responded, scrunching her eyes tightly, painfully ignoring her urge to open them.

'Okay, you can look now,' said Grigor, watching her as she spun around. Aphia twirled and opened her eyes simultaneously; she was both mesmerised and flummoxed by what she saw. The dirt track that led to the town had been completely refurbished. But not just restored, its appearance was as Aphia had envisioned on the day she and Grigor had first made their way to the cemetery. Aphia was speechless.

'I take it silence is good?'

'Who came up with the design? Who decided to pave with stones of all shapes and colours? Who planted the rhododendron hedges of red, pink and white? Can you hear the bee-eater birds? Listen, I can hear them from deep inside the rhododendron? You can hear them, can't you? Tell me you can hear them,' she repeated.

'Yes, I can hear them. Of course I can. You may not believe it but I came up with the design. You seemed so upset that day when I suggested you visit your grandmother's grave. You kept murmuring about rhododendron and honey and bee-eater birds and how you could hear the most wonderful tunes coming from the hedges. It was almost as if you believed it to be real. So I decided to make it real for you and here it is, your very own fairy tale entrance which, you will, of course, have to share with everyone else!' he laughed.

Aphia was overwhelmed by Grigor's sincerity. 'Come on,' she said, taking his hand. 'I feel like skipping down the road!'

'Well, I don't think skipping down the road is necessarily the right image for the Mayor but you go ahead. Skip all you like,' he said, humorously.

Aphia let go of his hand and skipped along the path to the tune of the bee-eater birds. Grigor powerwalked to catch up with her and hand in hand they entered the new entrance to the Language Town.

'Mother Tongue Citizens, as we stand here on the eve of the Language Town launch, I want to share with you how elated I am about our town's future. The last few months has been a journey I never deemed possible and all my dreams of securing our language, culture and way of life are about to come true. This Language Town will enable outsiders to come and sample our way of life and language! This Language Town will ensure that we remain an independent state and will generate income. This Language Town is being emulated in every district in our great nation and the whole world will come to know that we love our language, culture and each other. Most importantly, this Language Town continues the legacy set out by our beloved Apollos and Jakov that we do not need or will ever need to embrace Global to thrive or survive.

'So, tomorrow, we will see the first influx of tourists and I want to publicly declare that this has been our journey, our adventure and that we couldn't have done this without one another.

'Tomorrow and the day after that, let's ensure that each person who enters our town has the best experience a holiday could ever give. Let's ensure they leave telling their family, friends and neighbours that they also need to have a Language Town experience!'

Grigor was elevated by the rapturous applause from his citizens.

Aphia stood amongst the crowd; she loved being part of the community and left Grigor to the podium. After all, he was Mayor and she was taken aback by how confident he had become addressing the people.

Aphia looked around at the people cheering and clapping. Tomorrow would be an historical day for their town yet she felt extremely worried about Grigor's denial about the financial implications. He was certain that tourists would be clamouring to book a Language Town experience and this would give them the cash flow they needed.

The cheering and applause calmed down and Grigor announced, 'And, in true tradition, we have cake, lots of it, so please enjoy,' he continued, as his mother unveiled her latest ziggurat masterpiece to the delight of the crowd.

'Cake, who wants cake? A decent meal would be a nice change,' moaned a disgruntled citizen under her breath to her friend. 'I'm not sure how much longer we can survive? The men haven't had any wages for months and when I ask my husband "when are you being paid?" he gets defensive and mumbles "any day now." I don't understand why they are being so tolerant with the Mayor. We need money. What's the point of having this language town for tourists when the people who live here are poverty stricken? I'm going to speak up, now, while the whole town is here, while the Mayor is here. He can give us answers.'

'Your husband won't take too kindly to you embarrassing him! We are all in the same situation;

believe me. Give it a few more days and if the men still haven't been paid I will speak out with you. You have my word.'

Aphia watched dumbfounded as the women skulked away. She had no idea that Grigor hadn't been paying wages to the workers. She needed answers and quickly, before they had a riot on their hands.

'What are you doing?' demanded a very startled Grigor, as he discovered Aphia rifling through his office draws.

'Open this one,' she asserted, believing that the locked draw contained the financial information about which she had previously questioned Grigor.

'Aphia, you can't come in here like a thief in the night and snoop through official council papers. You can't insist on access to confidential financial records. That's why the draw is locked, for security reasons.'

'Grigor, just open the draw, I know about the debt. I know the men haven't been paid. I overheard the women. Are you aware that families within your town have no money for food?' she asked.

Reluctantly, Grigor unlocked the draw that contained the cost projections for the Language Town. He hesitantly handed the documents to Aphia.

Aphia pensively read the information and felt sickened by how much debt had been generated by creating the Language Town. She had no idea how they could recover.

'You watched me skipping down the road, like an excited teenager, celebrating the new entrance when you knew that your workers haven't been paid for months. Why Grigor? Why would you construct such an extravagant entrance while our own people are struggling.' Aphia was furious that Grigor had carried on with the Language Town structure. She was equally concerned that he seemed in denial of his reckless actions.

'Grigor, why didn't you tell me? I would have supported you.'

'No you wouldn't. You, like everyone else, would have told me that the Language Town was an impractical dream. I did not want to involve you, because, this way the problem is totally mine. The debt is totally mine. You are absolved of all blame.'

'But how are we going to rectify the situation?' 'I've taken care of it,' replied Grigor, solemnly.

'How?' she asked, concerned by his demeanour, believing that his actions were filling him with turmoil.

'In a few hours I will have the money needed to pay the workers and settle all the debt.'

'Not more borrowing, Grigor? Please tell me you haven't borrowed even more money?'

'No, no more borrowing. I've sold some of the town's assets.'

'What assets?'

'Just something that's been hanging around unused for years,' replied Grigor, vaguely. 'Something that the townsfolk don't need and nobody will really miss. When they realise that my aim is to safeguard the prosperity of our town they will forgive me.'

'Forgive you for what?' asked Aphia, feeling both alarmed and annoyed by his cryptic clues. 'What assets? What has the town got that is worth thousands upon thousands that they won't … land, it's land isn't it?'

'Yes,' replied Grigor, impassively.

'What land?' demanded Aphia, 'what land?'

Grigor made his way to the window and looked out at the greenbelt area.

Aphia stood by his side; she turned to him and was perturbed by the pain in his face. She, too, looked out of the window at the unspoilt panorama and gazed quizzically at Grigor. She had a queasy feeling in the pit of her stomach.

'Oh Grigor, what have you done? You have no right to authorise such a sale. It's protected. It's a greenbelt area. It contains endangered species,' she cried out in anguish.

'It's okay,' he said, reassuringly, taking her hand. 'You don't have to worry because the purchaser wants to build a school which will benefit our town and children. We can move the children out of the tin shacks into a brand-new building. I have dreamt of being able to give our youngsters a state-of-the-art school since becoming Mayor. Can't you see what a blessing this is? Not only can we use the money to settle all debt, but our townsfolk will also be earning money because the purchaser has agreed to employ our people to build the school. It's a true blessing, Aphia. Everyone wins. It will enable the town to prosper once more and, most importantly, ensure that the Language Town grows and Global is kept out.'

'But I don't understand. Who from outside our town would care enough to build a school for the children? How could you sell a piece of land that's protected habitat?'

'Because the Municipality's legislation states that the land can be sold, as long as it's not for commercial gain.'

Grigor produced the necessary document and there in black typeface was proof that the land could be sold and developed *only* if it were for educational purposes or if the town ever needed to use it as a graveyard.

'But Grigor, you should have come to me. I could have raised enough money to settle the debt.'

Grigor carried on seemingly oblivious to Aphia's comments that she could raise the money. Momentarily she pondered telling him the truth about her life in Global City and how her position at GSW had enabled her to buy a property which had escalated in value and was worth thousands upon thousands.

'Look, here, this will give you peace of mind. I have included guarantees that will ensure the species are rehoused in their respective environments. It's already arranged. Nothing will be harmed Aphia, you must trust me.'

'Who has bought the land? And what is in it for them? Who builds a school for free and pays the wages of the local community? This doesn't feel right to me, Grigor. Your eagerness to construct the Language Town has blinded you to potential duplicity!'

'An agent acting on behalf of the purchaser. I've had the endorsement of the Community Council.'

'May I see the purchase agreement?' asked Aphia, concerned with whom Grigor had been dealing.

'Of course,' he said, handing her the paperwork. 'This is the figure for which you sold the land?' 'Yes, it's an excellent price. Well above value.'

Aphia looked at Grigor dismayed that he and the Community Council naively believed the sum in question was adequate. She knew the real value of land. She had seen property prices in Global City and the Motherlands soar, making it impossible for the younger generation to purchase. Property owners were equally exploiting people by charging outrageous rents.

Aphia turned to the last page on the purchase agreement, to the signatory. What she saw made her squirm with unease. The signature was not a Mother Tongue name but a Global one; a name she instantly recognised - Rod Jones. Aphia was speechless that this was the second time she had encountered Rod Jones's influential signature. Rod's endorsement of Global Standard when he worked for the GSPC had earned him his GSW promotion and now it seemed that his loyalty to Stephen Law, as evident in this purchase, had pushed him further up the GSW ladder.

Aphia couldn't believe that Grigor had not entertained the possibility that, even though the legal document was in their Mother Tongue, the agent may have been a Global Citizen. His naivety was astounding. Aphia deliberated whether or not to tell him. She didn't know whether she should forewarn him that, despite his supreme efforts to keep GLOBAL OUT, his desperation had unwittingly and inadvertently let GLOBAL IN.

31

Angelina's parents were dismayed that she had returned home. They thought her and Rod's move to Global City was permanent and, harsh as it was for them, they resolved they would go to their graves without seeing their children again. They stoutly believed that life in Motherland was worth turning their backs on family, language and culture. They yearned for Rod and Angelina to have the best of everything and dreamt how their grand and even great grandchildren, would ensure that future generations of their family gained status and prosperity by being Global Citizens. Their conviction was that there was no longer any merit in being a Mother Tongue citizen and that Global City in Motherland was the only worthwhile place to live.

Angelina was equally as dismayed to be home. She was hurt by her parents' cold-hearted reaction on her return and had been shocked that her application for Global Citizenship had been declined. She had no idea why. The consequences of any refusal was the immediate receipt of an eviction notice to leave Global City. She was utterly confounded. After Rod had left to carry out his covert mission in Area Blue (which he had been forbidden to discuss with her) she felt abandoned and hadn't known how to proceed with her Global life. Despite her Global Standard proficiency (she had devoted hours to the Global Standard dictionary ensuring that her vocabulary was impeccable) she had been unable to secure employment. She had even considered approaching Stephen Law directly. She recalled her comment to Rod just before he left, "Maybe, I'll ask Mr. Law for a job," and how Rod had unwittingly given his approval. But Angelina's attempts to secure an appointment with Stephen had been in vain. Access to Mr. Law was prohibited via Claudia and contact with her was only obtainable through a number of GSW gatekeepers. Angelina's association with Rod did not afford her any special treatment and it certainly did not give her direct contact with Stephen Law.

In fact, when Claudia reported to Stephen that Angelina was requesting a meeting, he feared that she had made the connection between him and Nastan Popov. He recalled the intense vulnerability she made him feel at the Global Standard launch party.

"How dare these people interfere with the progression of my vision by unconsciously catching me off-guard?" he remembered thinking angrily. "These people," included Angelina. The trust he'd placed in her when he was a bereaved teenager now meant her potential realisation of his identity posed the biggest threat to his GS vision. She knew him as Nastan Popov and he had to eliminate her from Global City and his life to distance the risk.

Sadly, he had no idea that Angelina was intent on keeping their secret IF the RISE of Global was a blessing and not a curse and did not negatively impinge upon other nations or her brother. Only then would she speak up. She hadn't decided exactly what she would do, just merely watch and wait. She had no intention of reminiscing about the past, choosing to concentrate instead on her future in Global City.

Now that future had been denied her, she would have to determine her next course of action. After all, she considered herself to be a vintage Global speaker. She had most certainly been speaking Global for longer than any converts in Global City and the Motherlands - Stephen Law included. The irony was that Angelina had inadvertently set Stephen on his Global path, as it was with her that he practised speaking the language, as part of his therapy sessions.

But Stephen was not prepared to allow his past to dictate his future; a future that could very well be set off course by Angelina. To minimise possible exposure, she needed to leave Global City and return home, taking her knowledge with her.

"Just be careful. He can be very ruthless if you anger him," Rod had warned Angelina just before he left.

So Angelina surmised that Stephen's ruthless deportation was a sign of his anger. She did not realise that, instead, it was borne of fear. However, Angelina could not feel resentment towards Stephen because she remembered him as the sad, lonely teenager who had lost his only living relative. She reminisced about the teenage boy, who sat in the corner of a room singing along to the tune of Happy Birthday, his mouth out of sync with his own Mother Tongue because even then he was obsessed with Global. Fatalistically, she would accept his decision about her, but she needed to fill in the gaps of the last twenty years. She wanted to know how a boy from a small town background had established himself as the leader of the free Global world and how he had convinced world leaders to share that vision. She needed to trace his footsteps, starting from the time he spent at the International School. She believed that the only way to do this was by returning to where they had first met – their homeland. They shared a country, two languages and now, a secret.

32

‘You will not believe this email I’ve just received,’ said Penelope.

‘Try me,’ replied her colleague. ‘I’ll read it to you. Listening?’ ‘Always,’ he replied.

“Dear Global Daily Update. I am writing to you as a concerned Global Citizen. I have recently returned, well, actually, returned is probably not the right word. I was recently evicted from my holiday destination for – ‘you are not going to believe this’ – speaking Global Standard in the privacy of my hotel room! I booked a Language Town holiday experience in a Mother Tongue country. The whole idea seemed amazing, a real adventure, being able to learn the basics of another language while on holiday. I didn’t expect to come home fluent but I thought, wow, that’s a unique idea. None of my neighbours have had a Language Town experience. But I have never faced hostility like it. It’s almost unnatural.”

Penelope’s colleague interrupted her, ‘Is your correspondent talking about this country, Motherland? Isn’t that GSW’s real agenda?’ he said, sarcastically.

‘Very funny, GSW’s vision for Global Standard is grounded in economic and social reasons, but this seems obsessive. Anyway, I shall continue … .’

“On arrival at the Language Town I handed in all my devices. I knew this was expected of me because it’s the whole point of the holiday – full immersion from day one. I thought, this is going to be a really authentic experience. However, I needed to use the phone in my room to speak to my business colleague - in Global Standard as that’s our only shared vernacular. Anyhow, the following morning something remarkable happened. At breakfast I was given an eviction notice. I couldn't believe it. I thought it was a prank at first but this was a legal document. I had apparently shown a blatant disregard for the holiday rules. I was ordered to leave immediately and was escorted to the airport. I am looking into the legalities of this … ."

Penelope continued, 'The writer goes on to say that, as we are the oracle for all things Global Standard, she thought we would be interested in hearing about this. What on earth is going on in this Language Town? This is blatant prejudice against Global Standard!'

'As opposed to blatant prejudice against every other Mother Tongue in existence BY Global Standard, under the guise of GSW,' commented Penelope's colleague again.

'What do you have against Global Standard being spoken in countries that want it?' enquired Penelope.

'Why are you defending GSW when you are of Mother Tongue heritage? I thought you would be against GSW and everything it stands for. After your interview with Rod Jones you told me you needed to find "the teacher", the "mastermind" behind GSW. What happened to your hunch? Where has your urgency to tell the story gone? Why haven't you contacted Rod Jones to get an inside scoop?' he enquired, confused by this version of Penelope he hadn't seen before.

'Are you ashamed of your ancestry, that you hail from a minority people?' he quizzed her. 'Is that what's stopping you? Now you are living in Global City are you embarrassed that people will not accept you because you are not a native Global Citizen?'

'What? How dare you! You know nothing of the hardships of being a "minority people" as you put it. You were born privileged, Global speaking royalty. You didn't go to school in a shed and save scraps of Global newspaper cuttings from tourists who assumed you were uneducated and unintelligent just to try to learn the language. Did your parents work seven jobs between them to ensure you could leave your restricted community where only service jobs are available to natives, like hotel work, cleaning up after the Global elite? Don't you dare tell me I am ashamed of my heritage. I speak four languages. I can give you the meaning of words which go beyond your inherent understanding in Global, or its new variant, Global Standard. What's the difference in the two of them incidentally – a few spelling variations? It's still the most lacklustre language on the planet. But what do I know? How on earth, it's THE most revered language which everyone wants to speak is a mystery to me!'

'Finished?' he retorted.

Penelope glared at him, wondering if she'd gone too far? They were work friends but he was her superior.

'That's the hunger you had when you first started working for this channel. You had a voice that wanted to be heard. You had passion and opinions that really mattered but just like the rest of us you have, I'm afraid, become globalised. We have become too comfortable in our cosy Global world where we don't have to fight for anything any longer. We have grown lazy. We expect people to speak our language and if they don't we call them uneducated. Really, you should pity me with the Global spoon in my mouth. I would love to have what you have. I would love to have your knowledge; the skill to open my mouth and speak another language, to communicate with someone in a form that is so intrinsically linked to their culture that it seeps into the very essence of a person. Now that's a human bond. It's the type of salutation that morphs naturally into touch. I don't mean a false kiss on each cheek; a greeting that comes with a touch on the persons' arm that shows sincerity.

'What is Global Standard really? A stereotypical, plastic repetition. I saw it in Rod Jones. He was like a rehearsed mannequin when he came here that day. He uttered the right words and wore the right clothes. But was that really him? He was stripped of personality. When he gave his interview I saw what the future looked like as a Global Citizen - and I didn't like it.

'But I like what I hear when I listen to you. An ardent, astute Mother Tongue citizen unconfined by language.'

Penelope could feel tears coursing down her cheeks.

'Hey, no tears. I don't do tears. I'm Global, don't forget,' he smirked. 'Weakness will not be tolerated and all that!' he joked, handing her a tissue. 'I want you to take that passion, go to that country and find out what's going on there. But not just as a journalist, also as a Mother Tongue citizen. I want you to expose the truth.'

'But we are a news channel, we don't do truth,' said Penelope, sarcastically.

'We do now,' he replied, sincerely.

Penelope departed, with a new excitement; she had missed being out in the field. What she failed to disclose was the country which the disgruntled, Global Citizen had written about was her own. Admittedly, she had grown up in a different district to the Language Town but it was still her homeland. Penelope was extremely perplexed about the evident extremism. When she had migrated, her country was not like that. It welcomed tourists, whatever language they spoke. She needed to get to the truth behind this obsession with barring Global. Penelope needed to protect her homeland from accruing adverse publicity from this prejudice.

She was delighted that all these years later, she would be able to do something positive for her country. She would be able to repay her parent's diligence and hard work by reporting the truth. But, she was concerned that the cost of seeking the truth could result in renouncing her right to be a Global Citizen.

33

Penelope sat on the coach feeling guilt that her mother had no idea she wasn't returning to Global City. She hadn't told her family she was travelling to the other side of their country because they would have wanted to prolong their time together. They would have insisted on travelling with her and it would only have complicated the situation. Her family had stood, waving, smiling and crying tears of sadness and joy as she was driven away in the taxi, coach station bound.

As the coach reversed slowly from the bus terminal and backed up around the corner ready to embark on its journey, Penelope saw a woman on the kerbside flapping one arm frantically, while holding a suitcase and trying awkwardly to catch up with the coach. Penelope stood and instinctively yelled stop in Mother Tongue at the bus driver. The other passengers looked curiously at her as the driver brought the coach to a sudden halt.

'There's one more passenger,' she said somewhat embarrassed by the attention she was receiving. As she slunk into her seat, a very dishevelled Angelina clambered onto the coach, thanking the driver.

'Don't thank me,' said the driver, 'thank the yeller,' he remarked.

Not knowing who that was, Angelina collectively thanked and apologised to everyone on the coach and found a seat. She, too, was Language Town bound.

34

Aphia followed the path that led to the graveyard wondering what her mind had been doing that day when she imagined the wonderfully coloured stones, rhododendron hedges and honey-bee birds. But today, in stark contrast, there was no fairy tale scenery, just her and a path of dirt and stone. Despite Grigor's actions concerning money, now that Aphia was back in the habitat where she'd first imagined the fairy tale scenery, she realised that the new Language Town entrance was born out of Grigor's love for her.

The brambles had grown thicker since her last visit. She was relieved that she had borrowed an old walking stick she'd found in Grigor's office to push aside the thorny brambles. As she made her way to the clearing she thought of how her grandmother had supported her Global dreams. She doubted if her grandmother would be happy she'd returned home and married Grigor. She took a deep breath to console herself as she entered the cemetery.

"Agabus Demas, husband of Aphia Joan Demas, a much-loved husband, father and grandfather " she read poignantly. "Aphia Joan Demas – a much loved wife, mother and grandmother." A further inscription read:

"Surely it is not death that should flummox us, but God's grace that enables us to live until such a time that death gives us new life through Jesus".

As Aphia pondered these words and puzzled how death could give new life she was suddenly disturbed by the sound of wailing. She peered around and in the distance saw an old woman, dressed in black, hunched over a grave. Aphia felt overwhelmed by the pain this person was displaying, accentuated by her cries of anguish. The old woman seemed oblivious to Aphia's presence and continued crying, unashamedly. Moved by this public show of raw emotion, Aphia made her way to the distressed old lady. Aphia noticed that she was leaning on a walking stick similar to the one she had borrowed from Grigor's office. Unsure whether to disrupt her, Aphia stood and watched, hoping she would sense her presence. But as the minutes passed, Aphia backed away, relieved that the old woman hadn't noticed her. After all, she had her own grief to work out. As Aphia turned around to leave, the old woman stopped crying.

'I knew your grandmother. She was my best friend,' she called out.

'Excuse me?' said Aphia.

'Your grandmother was my neighbour for years. I blessed the day she came to live in our mountain village.'

'You knew my grandmother?' asked Aphia, excitedly.

'I said so, didn't I? You don't have to pretend either.'

'Pretend?'

'There's no need up here. There's no one around. You are free to speak Global. You are Aphia, aren't you?'

Aphia was dumbfounded and didn't know how to respond.

'I can hear it in your accent. My eyesight isn't good due to these lousy cataracts but my ears are simply fine. I heard you speaking to her, to your grandmother, apologising for leaving. Why would you apologise? That's an insult to her memory. She enabled you to leave. She wanted you to prosper. Have you prospered?'

'It's a long story,' Aphia replied, solemnly, wondering if she should explain that she wasn't apologising for leaving home but for abandoning Global City.

‘Well, I have all the time in the world,’ she responded. ‘You can begin with an explanation of why you are here,’ she said, commandingly, hoping that the sudden appearance of Aphia Joan would mean she would at last know the fate of Phoebe and Georgia. Maybe, just maybe, she could stop crying for a while.

‘Have you visited your grandmother’s home?’ she asked.

‘No, not yet. I can’t seem to bring myself to go.’ ‘Well it’s just as she left it. We make sure of that.’ ‘Sorry? Who makes sure of what?’

‘We are old but still able to ensure the house is aired and dusted. Your family don’t come up here anymore. Noadiah hasn’t visited since your grandmother passed away.’

‘How much do you know about me exactly?’ asked Aphia, anxiously.

‘I know it all. Well, everything up until your grandmother died,’ she said in Global.

‘Please, no Global,’ said Aphia, alarmed by the audacity that someone of her generation would converse in Global, knowing Grigor’s NO GLOBAL policy.

‘Why not? That’s the language you speak, isn’t it?’ ‘No, I am not that person any longer.’

‘So how are things in town? Is the Mayor still managing to keep Global out?’

Aphia fell silent and could feel her temperature rising. She very awkwardly placed her right hand over her left, covering her wedding band.

‘What? You don’t know? Don’t you have family who visit?’ continued Aphia.

‘No, not since my granddaughters, Phoebe and Georgia left. The rest of my family want nothing to do with me. They blame me for them leaving town. They blame your grandmother, too, but she isn't here to protest her innocence.'

'Phoebe is your granddaughter?' she uttered, amazed that her visit to the cemetery had enabled them to meet.

'Why do they blame my grandmother for your granddaughters leaving?'

'Because your grandmother ignited the Global spark with her stories of your life in Global City; my granddaughters were so enthralled with you and what Global City had to offer they left; first Phoebe, then Georgia. I haven't heard from either of them since they left.'

'Once you hear what I have to tell you, I am sure you will feel like rejoicing, not wailing,' said Aphia, emphatically.

'Then, after that, you can tell me how long you have been married to the Mayor,' she replied, shrewdly.

***

As Aphia left the mountain village she felt ecstatic that she had been able to give Phoebe's grandmother such amazing news about Phoebe's wellbeing. Sadly, she had not been able to confirm Georgia's whereabouts so tried to use reason to reassure her that if Phoebe had arrived safely in Global City, then why shouldn't Georgia too. As Aphia descended the slope that cut into the mountainside, she peered over her shoulder and could see her grandmother's house in the distance. As she stared, a light suddenly appeared in one of the windows. Then another room was illuminated until the whole house looked like a beacon on a hill. Aphia wiped away her tears, amazed that her grandmother's friends ensured her house did not look derelict. They kept it looking alive as they did her grandmother's memory. Aphia decided that she would like to visit her grandmother's home and hoped that Phoebe's grandmother would accompany her.

As Aphia walked down the steep trajectory, Phoebe's grandmother's words echoed repeatedly in her ears,

"I know better than to come between husband and wife. But you should tell Grigor the truth about your past before someone else does. It would be even more heart breaking hearing it from someone else. Beware of those closest to you. They often want to cause you the most trouble."

Her astute words made Aphia brood over Noadiah's earlier trickery. It was her sister's words that had convinced Grigor that Aphia was home sick for the mountain village. Of course, Aphia knew that Noadiah's comments had been referring to Global City and wondered if it was only a matter of time before her resentment of Aphia's return, would make her act further out of revenge. Noadiah had so wanted to join Aphia in Global City. Their grandmother's death had given her the freedom to leave, but, before she could, Aphia had foiled her plans. Noadiah needed Aphia to be in Global City to guarantee her full citizenship. Aphia's home coming had removed Noadiah's safe passage. Aphia concluded that Noadiah was definitely the person closest to her, most likely to cause the greatest trouble.

As Aphia mulled over the situation, she could see the museum building in the distance with the statue of Apollos outside. She recalled her conversation with Phoebe about how she had sparked the Global Wave generation in her town. How Aphia was secretly revered by the younger generation who wanted to leave. But Aphia did not feel any joy from being revered, just trepidation about the secrets she harboured. Aphia could not envisage how to remedy her personal situation without ruining her marriage and Grigor's life. She knew she had to tell him the truth, but the truth meant heartache and she didn't want her life with him to end. She had to think of a way to appease Noadiah until she was ready to tell Grigor. She would not be threatened by her sister.

35

Stephen stood on his balcony invigorated by the sight of the original neon sign which adorned the GSPC building opposite. He recalled how this emblem had instigated the "One Language, One Version, One Vision" mantra around Global City and now all Global Standard endorsed regions. As he stretched out his arms, the mourning doves perched lightly on his hands, one in each, foraging for seeds. Stephen breathed in slowly through his nose and exhaled through his mouth, rejuvenating his body. He felt a familiar chill engulf him which caused the doves to fly back to their perch.

'Stephen, Stephen, Stephen,' whispered a well-known voice in his ear. 'Many years ago when I purchased this land and building, enabling your Global Standard dream to come to fruition, you had no idea what we would achieve.' Stephen recalled that day vividly. He remembered the exciting, powerful aura to which he had been inexplicably drawn. He also shuddered when he recalled how the power his invisible ally conjured, could so easily turn to fear and dread ...

The day Stephen had been trapped in the lift at the GSPC building seemed like a lifetime ago.

The Invisible Stanger had set Stephen a task, "You will go to Norman's office and not leave until you have met with the commander-in-chief. Do you understand?"

So Stephen complied and turned up unannounced at the GSPC building. He made himself at home in Norman's office, waiting for the "real Director"; waiting for Norman's superior to seek him out. But, as time ticked slowly by, Stephen become increasingly annoyed that this person was seemingly ignoring his presence in the building.

He'd been equally vexed that he hadn't bypassed Norman a long time ago and met with his superior. But, the Invisible Stranger had reassured Stephen that when the time was right Norman would step out of the way, ushering in the next phase of Global Standard domination.

Ordinarily, Claudia, Norman's secretary, would have treated Stephen with respect, just like any other visitor. But when he had commandingly marched passed her into Norman's office, without even a thought that his very presence was polluting the very space where Norman's aged father had died, she determined that he would be oblivious to her. David knew he was in the building, so she left the matter in his hands. Watching Stephen's authority being chipped away, by being ignored, filled her with a wry satisfaction. He became increasingly frustrated at being kept waiting.

'Two hours,' he fumed to himself. 'Nobody disregards the leader of the free Global world,' he deliberated, whilst reasoning that the GSPC would not exist if it wasn't for his vision of a one world language.

When Stephen finally emerged from Norman's office, Claudia assumed he was leaving the building. However, David had known better and anticipated Stephen's next move - that he would seek him out. After all, with Norman absent from his duties who else would he have wanted to see?

David watched Stephen enter the communal lift and press the button for the final floor. David smirked, knowing that Stephen's quest was fruitless, as access to David's office was via a private lift, operated by a secret code that only he knew. As David contemplated the reason for Stephen's unannounced visit, an eerie high pitched noise seemed to be coming from his personal lift. Perplexed, he made his way to the elevator to investigate.

"Who are you?" David asked, alarmingly, as the lift door slid open and the Invisible Stranger appeared. "How did you access this lift?"

"Let's just say my name is Stephen Law."

David knew this person was not Stephen Law, because Stephen was in the staff lift trying to figure out how to get to his office. An inexplicable fear gripped David which was exasperated by the eerie presence of this stranger.

"No. Stephen Law is … ," David replied, feebly. "David, David, David," the Invisible Stranger interjected.

"Whether I am Stephen Law, or I represent Stephen Law does not really matter. We need to discuss the Norman situation. This is what is going to happen … ."

David felt compelled to listen, mesmerised by the hypnotic voice of the Invisible Stranger. Listen was all he could do, as, bizarrely, his vision had blurred and he was unable to clearly see the stranger's face. The immaculate black suit standing before him issued instructions that Norman was to be kept on the payroll. He was also to keep all his GSPC credentials but, significantly, Norman was to be just a decoy. A much needed distraction. The reason why, the stranger did not say.

Stephen's experience of being in the GSPC building become very surreal. He wasn't used to not being in control. On entering the lift, it started climbing slowly upwards but plummeted sharply downwards, coming to an abrupt halt. The door remained firmly shut. He pressed the emergency button and shouted into the intercom, demanding help, but nobody came to his assistance.

"Let me out," Stephen barked into the intercom again and again, his cries being obscured by a disturbing high-pitched scraping. As the lift door slowly slid back, Stephen was faced with complete darkness and heard the static of an open communication line.

"Stephen, Stephen, Stephen," a voice muttered, relentlessly.

"Who are you? Who's there?" Stephen shouted frantically, feeling very unnerved.

"Come, come Stephen. Surely you recognise the voice of your loving guardian angel?"

Stephen didn't feel comfort from the presence of the voice that was more than familiar to him.

"Show yourself, show yourself," Stephen yelled into the darkness, in a frenzied state.

"Mr. Stephen Law, Mr. Stephen Law, Mr. … ," another voice interjected calmly. "At last I've found you," said David, quite casually. As he continued speaking, the darkness was illuminated by the lighting system of the basement.

"You seem to have become quite lost. I'm sorry that you have been kept waiting. I am David, Norman's boss. Let's go to my office so we can discuss the situation regarding Norman … ."

Coming back to his senses, Stephen knew the brooding presence was right. He had aided Stephen to become the leader of the free Global world and hadn't asked for anything in return. He was enabling Stephen to fulfil his ambition in the name of Global Standard and in memory of his late father. Stephen owed him his loyalty and he would ensure that he adhered to the hazy silhouette's instructions for spreading Global Standard to the ends of the world. No one would stand in the way of their plans, most certainly not, Norman.

36

'Good morning Mr. Mayor,' Mother Tongue citizens and tourists alike said cheerily to Grigor as he paraded around the town sporting his chain of office.

'Mr. Mayor, please,' a tourist urged him, indicating her request for a photograph. Grigor beamed with pride as he stood in the centre of her family's holiday picture. Granted, this lady had only been able to utter a few words in his Mother Tongue, but it was enough to cause his heart to swell. After the photograph, Grigor took the camera from the lady in a jovial manner and taught her the word for camera in his language. As she repeated the word until she got the pronunciation correct, she prompted her family who also started to say the word over and over.

'Very good,' Grigor praised them in Mother Tongue and indicated to their Language Host to take over. As the family walked away, repeating the word and practicing others they had learnt, Grigor was elated.

'Mr. Mayor, please may I have a photograph with you to show my family when I return home,' asked another holiday maker in Mother Tongue. Grigor was more than willing to oblige and was impressed with the linguistic skills of the tourist. This was the proof he needed that his vision for the Language Town was worthwhile. As he walked around the town he was overjoyed that the only language he could hear was his own.

The townsfolk wearing their national dress looked like they were playing roles in a film. The citizen's houses were whitewashed and guest accommodation was painted in different pastel shades. The sky was blue, the birds were singing and his life as Mayor was complete. The town was prospering financially and all the debt had been paid off thanks to his insight and business acumen in selling a piece of greenbelt that was, quite frankly, not maximising its potential. The protected species had been rehoused on adjacent sites so he really did not have anything about which to feel guilty. Everything he had promised Aphia regarding the preservation of the green belt had been upheld. Grigor was looking forward to the future; a future which would give their town a much needed new school and its citizens more work than they ever dreamed possible.

Another tourist asked him for a photograph and he said, 'There's someone else who needs to be in the picture. Give me one minute and then you can snap away.'

As Grigor returned with Aphia he said proudly, 'Now you may take the photograph. Now it is complete.'

Aphia smiled outwardly but inwardly she remembered how she had felt on her wedding day - like a fraudster, a fake who didn't belong. As the flash from the device caused her to squint she thought she glimpsed Stephen Law standing in the crowd. She blinked and looked again and saw the same image. He was standing further back than most and was holding a different device to the others. She stared intently and thought she saw him taking her photograph with her mini pc; the one she had deliberately left behind in Global City.

Grigor thanked the crowd for their kindness and they dispersed with their allocated Language Hosts. As Aphia's vision cleared, she realised yet again, that she was imagining Stephen. She was wilting under the burden of her secret. Plus, she was still waiting for the ramifications of Rod Jones's purchase of the greenbelt. One thing was certain, he had purchased the land on behalf of Stephen Law. Aphia's heart ached terribly about the situation and she knew it was only a matter a time before her visions of Stephen in Area Orange turned into reality.

37

As the bus entered the last leg of its journey to the Language Town, Angelina sat at the front chatting to the driver and Penelope sat at the back taking in every inch of the scenery. Penelope had never visited this region of her homeland before, whereas Angelina had, albeit a long time ago.

'So how long is it since you've been here?' the bus driver asked Angelina.

'I was a graduate, hungry for life. I'll leave you figure it out.'

'You have a lot of catching up to do with your friends, eh?'

'Yes, a lot,' said Angelina, realising that friends wasn't quite the description of the people she was visiting.

'It's a good job you are a native,' commented the bus driver.

'Why?' asked Angelina, jovially?

'Because of the Language Town rules. You don't know?' he queried, observing Angelina's puzzled face.

'Well you are about to find out,' he said, approaching the new road that led to the gated entrance.

'What on earth?' said Angelina, mesmerised by the sight of the brightly coloured brick road and the grand design in the distance.

'Here,' said Penelope, who had made her way to the front of the bus for a better look. 'The details are in this brochure. I'm a native too, just here for the whole Language Town experience,' she clarified.

'Thank you.'

'She's your yeller,' confirmed the driver.

'You stopped the bus for me?'

'My pleasure. I'm Penelope, pleased to meet you.' 'Angelina, likewise.'

'Here you go ladies, enjoy your stay,' said the driver, pulling into the coach park.

'Have you been to this area before?' asked Penelope. 'Many years ago, but it didn't look like this,' replied Angelina.

'It's my first time. I live in the city and thought an authentic, cultural break would do me good. See you on the other side,' said Penelope making her way confidently to the checkpoint.

'Yes, see you … ,' muttered Angelina, anxiously, '… on the other side.'

38

'Mr. Mayor,' Grigor heard a Mother Tongue voice call after him.

He turned to see Penelope beaming a smile and holding out her right hand to formally greet him.

'Mr. Mayor, I cannot believe what you have achieved in our country. Oh, my apologies, I would like to introduce myself. My name is P… aloma and I am so pleased to meet you.'

'Likewise,' replied Grigor, courteously. 'Paloma; now that is a traditional name.'

'Yes it is. I was named after my great-grandmother; a tradition that I am pleased to say is being upheld in our country.'

'Yes, names are so important within families. How else will the generations recognise who they are if we stop handing down family names? What region are you from? I don't recall seeing you in our town before,' quizzed Grigor.

Feeling like an imposter and worried that her Global Standard accent had pre-eminence over her Mother Tongue's, she thought very carefully before speaking to ensure she sounded as native as Grigor. Penelope pictured herself in her parent's home with her siblings. She imagined the sound of their Mother Tongue chatter as they went about their daily activities. She heard the colloquialisms that formed part of their very essence and only a Mother Tongue citizen would understand. As Penelope conversed with Grigor about the region from which she originated, she grew in confidence. As Grigor nodded and laughed at Penelope's childhood stories, to which he himself could relate. The informal barrier between them was broken and they felt like old friends.

'It's really refreshing to hear such stories of childhood. I have spent so many years ensuring that our identity is protected that I sometimes forget how wonderful it is to be raised here. Why would anyone want to leave all this?' he mused, making an elaborate gesture with his hands.

Feeling ashamed that she couldn't fully agree with Grigor's statement, because she had left her homeland, Penelope asked, 'Protect? Why would we need protection?'

'Why from Globalisation of course. This is the purpose of the Language Town. The protection of our way of life and the right to speak our language in our own country, free from outsiders introducing legislation that will suppress our rights. Do not underestimate the impact other people's ideas may have on your own life, Paloma. Some ideas are genuinely for the greater good but some are not. We must ensure that we stay aware from all Global risks to our society. The biggest threat to our culture is the eradication of our language. I made a promise a long time ago to my Mayoral predecessor, committing myself to the preservation of Mother Tongue and this Language Town is the security blanket that covers us all. In fact, it won't be long until you'll be able to experience a Language Town in your own region,' said Grigor, proudly.

'In my own region? How?' Penelope asked, intrigued.

'Because each district within our country will emulate this Language Town; this will ensure that Mother Tongue is protected and Global is distanced. Global will never form part of who we are as a nation.'

'I truly look forward to that day,' said Penelope with sincerity. 'May our country prosper and our language live forever,' she said – unwittingly sounding like a true Mother Tongue fanatic.

'My sentiments exactly. In fact, how wonderful that would read on a plaque as a mantra for all to see! We could put … .'

Interrupting the Mayor's thoughts, Penelope asked, 'Could I have a photograph with you to show my folks at home?'

'Most certainly; but if you don't mind waiting for just one minute you can have a photograph with Mrs Mayor, too,' said Grigor laughing, spotting Aphia in the distance. 'It's a pleasure to meet you, Mrs Mayor,' said Penelope to Aphia as they shook hands amiably.

'Smile,' said Penelope jovially as a Language Host took the picture.

'How long are you staying in town?' asked Aphia. 'A few days,' she replied. 'I hope we get the chance to speak again.'

'Yes, I'm sure we will,' said Aphia, wondering why Penelope from Global Daily Update was visiting their town and pretending to be someone named Paloma. Aphia was flummoxed by Penelope's Mother Tongue identity. As a newsreader on the biggest Global channel in the Motherlands, Penelope's Global was flawless. Aphia assumed she was a Global native. Yet, here she stood, conversing in Mother Tongue with Grigor, like a pair of old school friends.

'I will look out for you around town,' said Aphia, 'maybe we could have a chat over coffee.'

'I'll look forward to it,' replied Penelope, unaware that Aphia was Joan Marsh and that she knew Penelope's true identity.

As Penelope walked away she pressed the stop button on the covert camera hidden in her jacket lapel. She couldn't wait to download the footage to her computer to review her interview with the Mayor. The photograph was the icing on the cake!

Aphia was concerned about Penelope's presence in the Language Town and wondered if Stephen Law had sent her? She desperately needed to know but couldn't risk revealing her own identity; after all, they had never met in Global City. Penelope's fame as a television newsreader made her a publicly recognisable figure within Global City. Aphia was certain that Penelope did not know her as Joan Marsh. She needed to ensure she bumped into Penelope again before she left town.

39

'Are you entering?' the Language Guard asked Angelina impatiently.

'Yes, my apologies,' she responded, realising she had been lingering for quite some time.

'I am a Mother Tongue citizen. Here is my identity,' interposed Angelina, handing over her passport.

'Do you have any Global literature or devices to declare?' he demanded sternly.

'No,' she replied defensively.

The guard inspected her credentials and looked at Angelina intensely. After what seemed like a long silence and after completing numerous tasks on his computer he declared, 'You may enter,' and opened the turnstiles which allowed her access into the Language Town.

As Angelina pushed the barrier tentatively she did not recognise the town which she had visited many years ago. Unable to process the new scenery she tried to remember the area as it was. She endeavoured to evoke a sense of nostalgia, feeling fearful that the unfamiliarity would force her to forget the importance of her visit. She had not expected to be battling with old and new. She had planned her itinerary meticulously. She would visit Nastan's and Grigor's homes and speak with Grigor's parents concerning Nastan.

'I will recognise Grigor's parents for sure,' she had thought positively, not even considering the possibility that they could have died since she saw them last, 'and they will be happy to see me and tell me everything I need to know concerning Nastan.'

But a sudden dread filled Angelina because she remembered how hostile Grigor's mother, Dorcas, in particular, had been to her because she had introduced Global into her home. She had brought a language into their lives of which they did not approve. Angelina had encouraged Nastan to communicate in Global. In fact, for the months that she had supported Nastan he had excelled in his pursuit of Global, learning new words and phrases daily to impress her. The realisation of how much she had influenced Nastan made her very uneasy and she wondered what welcome she would receive. During that time, Nastan and Angelina only spoke Global because, after Apollos' death, Nastan refused to communicate in Mother Tongue. Angelina shuddered as she remembered how she had enabled him to communicate in a language of which his grandfather and also his best friend, Grigor and his family, had disapproved.

Now many years later she had returned to this community where all her years of hard work and sacrifice learning Global meant nothing. She looked around at the Language Hosts in their national costumes. She observed the tourists' endeavour to speak a language that was not their own. She felt like an intruder in a country where she did not belong, except this was her homeland and she should have felt at ease.

Angelina looked up at the mountains that surrounded the town and remembered that Nastan's house was at the top of a hill. She slinked away from the bustle of the town square, deciding that, at the very least, she would visit Nastan's home before she left.

She walked slowly up the hill that led to the home Nastan had shared with his grandfather, Apollos. She remembered how Nastan would sprint up the hill, leaving her behind.

As she approached the top of the hill, Nastan's house came into view. Except it wasn't Nastan's home any longer. It bore no resemblance to the place she had visited many, many times. When it had belonged to Apollos it needed renovation, something that the new owners had obviously addressed. The rusted, creaky gate had been replaced with a brand new wooden one. The garden swing, that had been made from a plank of wood and a rope full of notches had been replaced. The whitewashed exterior and the sea-blue shutters evoked a tasteful blend of old and new. Angelina was mesmerised by this new version of a house that held so many memories of the beginning of her own working life.

Nastan had been the first child that she'd cared for in her role as bereavement councillor. She shuddered at the memory of leaving him at the International School as a bereft teenager. She remembered how she had cried in worry for him and his future. For some reason, she felt equally as concerned now, despite his maturity to adulthood with a mind capable of making independent decisions.

'He left a long time ago,' she heard a voice from behind her utter in Mother Tongue. 'Why have you returned? Why have you come here today of all days? Have you declared your allegiance to Mother Tongue or are you here to spy about the opening of the Language Town?'

She whisked around to come face to face with Grigor's mother. Her voice sounded angry but her face was stoic.

In their common language, Angelina replied, 'I have not come here to represent Global, if that's what you think. I have come here because I have a lot of loose ends concerning Nastan Popov.'

'Loose ends,' she mocked, 'loose ends,' she repeated, sounding regretful. 'Nastan Popov has not been seen nor heard of since the day you willingly abandoned him at the International School. Thanks to your misguided loyalty you encouraged a boy you hardly knew to fulfil an ambition that should have been dismissed. We've lived each day knowing how much we let down our beloved Apollos. We should have taken better care of Nastan. He should be here now with Grigor. They should have made this journey together. He should be here and you are not welcome.'

'You cannot hold me responsible for Nastan Popov. I was just doing my job. It was my duty to support him in his grief and Global gave him a purpose. I did not know that he would never return home.'

'You should have realised that he was obsessed with Global and losing Apollos fuelled his ambition. You should have discouraged his desire to be someone of whom Apollos would have disapproved. You should have encouraged him to stay at home with us. He had no idea who he was and we, now, have no idea where he is. I have grieved for him all these years. I repeat, you are not welcome here. You should leave before Grigor sees you. I do not want him upset today.'

'But Grigor is Mayor! Isn't that what he always wanted? Isn't that what you prepared him for since he was a teenager?'

'Just leave, you have no place here, language traitor.'

'Are you certain Grigor doesn't know where Nastan is?' asked Angelina. 'Are you sure this elaborate quest to keep Global out isn't because of Nastan? Maybe you should ask Grigor what he is most worried about? Or who?'

'What do you mean? This Language Town has nothing to do with Nastan. It is to revere Apollos and our deceased Mayor, Jakov. My husband and Grigor made them a promise to uphold our Mother Tongue.'

'But why this town? Why this country? Global is spreading at a rapid rate and most countries are welcoming the benefits. Why is our country so opposed to Global? Is it Global or the person who is spearheading Global to whom Grigor is most opposed?'

'You are making no sense. What person? The only person who posed a threat to our Mother Tongue being replaced with Global died many years ago, along with his plans,' retorted Grigor's mother, realising that she had divulged too much information.

'I can remember one day vividly,' recalled Angelina, 'it was Nastan's birthday and you'd made a magnificent cake. But Nastan sat in the corner of the room while everyone sang Happy Birthday. He sang along, sullenly, but he was singing in Global. I can remember how odd his lips looked because they were out of sync with everyone else's.'

'You brought Global into his life,' accused Grigor's mother.

'I did not. Global already existed. Someone else sparked his Global fascination long before I came to town,' said Angelina, protesting her innocence. 'Who was it? Who would have had such an influence over him?'

'I do not know what you are talking about. Go back to your Global life and never return. There is nothing here for you. There are no secrets waiting to be uncovered. The facts are simple. Nastan, in his grief, clung to the wrong person and wrong idea and left our lives for good. Maybe one day he will return and explain where he has been. But that's it. There is no mystery to be solved. Just intense regret that I did not uphold my promise to his grandfather.

I merely pray that wherever he is in the world he is happy and prospering.'

Angelina watched despondently as Grigor's mother, Dorcas walked away dismissively. She couldn't help but feel saddened that Dorcas had blamed herself for Nastan's departure from their home. Dorcas' harsh words made Angelina even more determined to ensure that Nastan resumed his original identity and his Stephen Law persona would cease to exist. Grigor's mother was right. She did not belong here. She belonged in Global City with her brother. Despite being deported she was determined to regain entry and be there for Nastan when his world falls apart as it had done all those years ago.

***

'Leaving so soon?' the coach driver asked Penelope.

'Yes. I've seen everything I came to see,' she replied, jovially.

Penelope sat at the rear, in the same seat as on her inward journey. She set up her device to play back her covert interview with Grigor. She couldn't wait for her broadcast to go live.

'You too? Leaving so soon?' said the driver to Angelina as she rushed onto the bus.

Wondering to what he was referring she replied, 'Just a flying visit.'

She decided that she would return to her parent's home to collect her belongings but then she would be Global City bound. How she would regain entry she didn't know, but Global City was the only place she needed to be.

40

'Sir, Area Purple is the latest to swear allegiance to Global Standard. I have instructed shipping to prepare the Translation Device order. Would you like to watch the live streaming of their Sovereign State's Mother Tongue renouncing ceremony?' enquired the Head Language Monitor. She had been elated when Stephen Law had selected her as Rod's understudy.

'No, I'm sure the Language Monitors have it under control. Just alert me if there are any problems,' replied Stephen, succinctly.

'Very well, Sir,' she replied, awaiting Stephen's next command.

'You may leave,' ordered Stephen.

Stephen purposefully swiped the purple hue and replaced it with black, confirming yet another Global Standard victory. Black was the label that symbolised the RISE of Global Standard throughout the world. Stephen retrieved his paper copy of the GSW world map and his father's original map from his briefcase and placed them on the conference table. He laid the GSW map on top of his father's and secured their alignment. He looked at the morphed image in glee as the purple was overwhelmed by the stark black colour. He looked broodingly at his own country's vibrant orange. It was yet to be globalised. He thought poignantly about his father's original idea for Global replacing their own Mother Tongue which still hadn't come to fruition. Stephen had chosen Area Blue as the prototype from which he could globalise all other countries. The black on the GSW map was spreading rapidly. But it still wasn't enough. His achievements meant nothing if his own country remained unchanged.

Stephen shifted his focus to another globalised region, Area Red. He looked at this conquest with burning intensity. The red hue mirrored the madness in Stephen's own eyes.

He summonsed the Head Language Monitor back to his office.

'How many citizens have passed the Global Standard Language Test in Area Red?' he asked forcefully.

'Area Red have purchased two million translation devices which is a huge victory, as the population is an aging one,' she replied, believing the revenue would fill him with satisfaction.

'I didn't ask how many devices have been sold. I asked how many people have passed the Global Standard Language test?' barked Stephen.

Realising that money wasn't his priority, she nervously collated the data from her mini pc, knowing that the result wouldn't be to his liking, 'roughly 0.02%,' she responded, timidly.

'0.02%; let's think about that figure for a moment, shall we?' growled Stephen rhetorically. 'Two million devices you say, which is of course excellent revenue for GSW and the GSPC. Plus, that's two million people renouncing their Mother Tongue in favour of Global Standard,' continued Stephen while she nodded her head emphatically in agreement.

'But, despite these "excellent" facts and figures, out of two million people, only four hundred have actually passed the Global Standard language test. Tell me, are these likely to become fluent in Global Standard or are they just device users? Are the "four hundred" now Language Monitors in this region, enforcing Global Standard or have this token number slipped back into their vernacular?'

She looked furtively at Stephen observing how the redness in his eyes had become tinged with purple; his gestures became more elaborate and his face seemed to grimace as if in pain.

'And here?' challenged Stephen, ranting, pinpointing another globalised region on the GSW world map.

'0.01 per cent,' she replied, sheepishly. 'But this region's government … .'

'Enough,' shouted Stephen, whilst simultaneously placing his left hand over his heart. The shooting pains had intensified over the last few weeks.

'I have heard enough excuses. I don't care how much revenue the licences are generating. I don't care how much profit we and the GSPC are making. All I care about is how many people across the planet are conversing in Global Standard. That is THE ONLY figure in which I am interested. Do you hear me?' he almost shrieked. 'Now go and do your job before I find someone else who can. Go and be my Language Warrior or do I need to retrieve Rod Jones from Sister Motherland to show you how it's done.'

'No, Sir, that won't be necessary.'

'Do not return until you have turned license holders into actual Global Standard communicators!'

She left feeling extremely chastised and had no idea how to fix this problem. 'I am not a teacher,' she thought begrudgingly, 'Mr. Law should be reprimanding the educationalists who designed the gadget. After all, they are apparently some of the best minds in the world.'

The academics who worked in the Secret Room had reassured Mr. Law that the simplicity of the design meant that the machine itself would be the teacher, converting Mother Tongue speakers into proficient Global Standard communicators within eight weeks.

But worst of all, she felt completely alone and had no one to whom she could turn in Global City. Stephen Law had made her sign a confidentiality agreement forbidding discussion of the Secret Room or any other details with anyone, including Rod. She didn't know why she couldn't seek his advice. They were colleagues, it just didn't make sense.

Rod felt equally isolated and Stephen's dominance over him was stronger than ever. Rod had no idea where Angelina was. He had hoped that his purposeful failure in Sister Motherland meant expulsion from his roles as Language Warrior and the face of GSW. He was prepared to accept his fate and hopefully this would allow him to leave and return home as he had desired for months. Yet, Stephen had not reprimanded him and had insisted he stayed in Sister Motherland as his second-in-command. Rod knew that this was in fact Stephen's silent reprimand.

As Stephen looked at the orange hue of his own country he felt anew the pact that he had sworn to himself years ago that, one day, he would return home and make his city the capital of Global. His headquarters there would be in an edifice so fine that it would reach up to heaven itself and every eye would see it and all people from every nation would aspire to emulate it. It would house one superpower, one super language: Global Standard, THE LAW. Global Standard would be spoken by all citizens of the world, under a new world order, which would be attributed to his late father's memory and of course, himself. His decision to move his headquarters to his hometown instead of the city had been incited by the fact that he wanted his name to be known from where he originated. He wanted his hometown to revere him and his father's legacy. Once he had globalised his hometown, he would take his vision to the city and from there take over the whole country.

He dialled a number on his mini pc which was rapidly answered by the recipient.

'Has the money been transferred for the purchase of the land?'

'Yes, Sir,' the voice replied. 'Everything is ready to proceed as planned.'

'Excellent,' said Stephen, feeling his spirit calm. He dialled Rod's mini pc and also summonsed his Head Language Monitor to attend his office immediately.

Rod answered and was shocked to see Stephen sitting at his desk, seemingly in a tranquil mood.

The Head Language Monitor was equally as surprised that the chaos of Stephen's office a few minutes ago had dissipated.

Stephen stood and walked over to his virtual wall map. Rod watched in trepidation at which country he would be tasked with globalising.

'Prepare to advance in the name of Global Standard,' said Stephen, authoritatively.

Rod looked at the hue to which Stephen was pointing and felt extreme agitation as realisation dawned that the next country to be dominated was Rod's own, Area Orange.

'Rod Jones, your time in Sister Motherland is complete. The Prime Minister has everything under control. I have sent instructions to your mini pc. You are to leave Sister Motherland immediately and go to Area Orange; here history will be made and you will be proud to be a part of it.'

Rod nodded in compliance. 'Here we go again,' he thought despairingly knowing that Sister Motherland had been the precursor for globalisation in his hometown, and the worst was yet to come.

41

Live on air in three, two, one …

'Welcome to Global Daily Update,' began Penelope. 'As Global Citizens we have passionately embraced the One Language, One Version, One Vision ideology of GSW and the GSPC. We have fully immersed ourselves in what it is to be a Global Citizen. In addition to this, GSW's mantra that Global Standard will become the common language of the world is being embraced by Mother Tongue leaders across the world, who have willingly renounced their vernacular in favour of Global Standard. It seems that most of the world's population is more concerned with the convenience of communicating and trading in one common language than remembering their origins. These convert countries are supporting GSW and the GSPC by, not only turning their backs on their native language, but by changing their country's name to Sub Motherland Region 5, 6, 7… whichever number is available.

'In fact, as more countries join the Global Standard Unification Act (GSUA), there is a clamour amongst those original converters over the date which they joined to ensure they are bestowed the correct region number. Why is the number so important? – because, in this instance the lower the number, the bigger the reward, especially for those regions in the top fifty - not a very egalitarian start to sharing an ideology and language.

'As each conversion country buys into GSW's dogma in favour of Global Standard, another Mother Tongue is in danger of extinction. Consequently, a country's culture and identity risk becoming obsolete in the name of Global Standard.

The introduction of the freedom of movement legislation, sanctioned by the Global Standard Unification Act, enables people to migrate from their own to a host GSUA country and become a Global Citizen. There are just two qualifying criteria: firstly, pass the Global Standard Language Test, referred to as the GSLT and secondly, renounce their Mother Tongue in favour of Global Standard. Global Citizens are then able to work and live in any of the GS regions belonging to the GSUA. This is the purpose of the GSUA; membership means citizens can leave their own country and work and live in any GSUA accredited region.

'So, how are non-native GS speakers passing a rigorous language test? Good question! The countries who belong to the GSUA have invested heavily in GSW's Global Standard Translate Technology which enables an adult Mother Tongue citizen to learn and pass the GSLT in just eight weeks. I have made a separate report on the impact the new law has on Mother Tongue children which I will share with you in tomorrow's Global Daily Update. Failure is not an option in the ideology of GSW and Citizens are supported by Language Monitors in their respective regions until citizens are accredited with Global Standard language success.

'For people who do not live in a GSUA country, there is an option to purchase the translation device as an individual. These individuals are highly favoured by GSW and the GSPC and most of the time the devices are given free of charge as a reward for their loyalty to the vision of Global Standard. But the consequence of this reward is conflict between their Mother Tongue country, GSW and the GSPC because, not all nations share the GS vision and some are, in fact, opposed to their citizens learning Global Standard. GSW and the GSPC are making the translation device available at a nominal cost to whoever wants it, regardless of that country's language policy. Exacerbating this situation, is the GSW's Relocation Programme where those labelled "language traitors" by *their* own government are given a free pass to live and study in Global City. In some cases, this is causing a diaspora from native homelands which, of course, impacts on family, culture and economies. It's becoming problematic for countries outside the GSUA who want to retain their language, citizens and work force. GS citizens are advantaged by being issued with a Global Citizen identity card affording them freedom of movement to travel as and when they choose.

'Oh you may ask, what's wrong with that? Isn't that the most efficacious use of people's skills? Plus, doesn't it ensure that all GSUA countries have the right worker for the right job? Well, to an extent I agree but, what about Mother Tongue citizens who want to stay in their country and speak their own language? Why should these people be ostracised and excluded? Why should they feel like they are being left behind and punished for not towing the Global Standard line? Shouldn't the same freedom afforded to GS citizens be extended to them - to cling to their heritage rather than relinquish it, if they so choose?

'I have recently returned from a Mother Tongue region where the Mayor is actively safeguarding his country's history. He is exercising every shred of his power to ensure his home town does not convert to Global Standard. In fact, he wasn't even aware that Global had been superseded by Global Standard. So how is he achieving this? The Mayor has pioneered a Language Town – the first of its kind in the world. The Language Town FORBIDS Global. There is a NO GLOBAL policy which has been in place for several years, long before the

Language Town was created. Surprisingly, the people who spend money on this holiday not only want to experience learning a new language but want to be free from Global Standard.

'I had the privilege of interviewing the Mayor and this is what he said …'

"A long time ago I made a promise to my predecessor that our nation would uphold its Mother Tongue. When we realised we were under threat from Global I decided to introduce a NO Global policy. We do not allow Global to be spoken anywhere in our town or indeed our country. It forms no part of our education, health or legal systems. With the aid of translation devices, Language Hosts and rudimentary symbols and words, visitors leave Global behind at the Language Town checkpoint. For the duration of their stay, the only language in which they converse or which they hear is Mother Tongue. The feedback we have had has been outstanding!"

'So viewers,' continued Penelope, 'this is how the language town functions … .'

As Penelope sat back and perused the film she had shot of her holiday in Area Orange she had no idea that Mr. Law was watching her broadcast from GSW headquarters. He made a point of viewing Penelope's programme every day as she had impressed him with her coverage of the Global Standard launch.

But, this time, Stephen watched in incredulity as he had a guided tour of his hometown. He observed in dismay as Penelope walked from street to street showing Mother Tongue citizens in their national dress.

Penelope's voiceover continued, 'Every day, the people adorn their national costume to ensure that holiday makers have an authentic experience. Tourists are encouraged to join in and this is the symbol system which allows them to communicate in Mother Tongue. This is how it works,' she said, pressing a sunshine symbol on the interactive device.

'So, when I press the sun symbol, Good Morning in Mother Tongue can be heard from the machine. I also have this portable handheld device which enables me to learn as I walk around. Let me show you,' she continued and pressed the food symbol.

'I know you are probably wondering how a Global speaker has been able to bring you this news report. Well, it's time for my confession … I am an Area Orange Mother Tongue native so I was able to conduct the interview with the Mayor in the town's own language.

'As Global Citizens you are probably wondering why I seem to be advocating speaking another language. The explanation is quite simple. Languages are fundamental to our origins. They confirm who we are and from where we have come. But there is another point that I would like to make. We do not need to eliminate one language in favour of another to be able to communicate cross culturally - something I have learnt from the Language Town. Yes, I can speak Area Orange's language, but, while I was there I communicated with people from all over the globe by smiling, laughing and using gestures.

'What's happened?' asked Penelope, quickly removing her earpiece that was suddenly making a staccato, scraping nose.

'We're off air,' said her producer dismayed. 'The whole building has lost power. Stay there while I find out what's going on.'

Penelope sat waiting for the green light which indicated she was on air to reappear. She was annoyed that she hadn't got to finish her report just as she was getting to the crux of the message.

‘Is that you, Lionel?’ she asked, feeling a cold breeze brush past her body. ‘Lionel, are you there? Where’s everyone gone?’ she asked alone in the murky studio.

As she sat in the darkness she heard a faint, high pitched noise. She got up and stumbled around trying to follow the sound. She soon realised the disturbing noise was still coming from her earpiece. She put it on and sat back down, thinking that the technical team were trying to communicate with her.

‘Hello, are we back on air?’ she asked, tentatively.

As she waited for a response she could hear the static of an open communication line.

‘Iona, Iona, Iona,’ she thought she heard in the distance. She was puzzled who would know her Mother Tongue name. The voice made her shudder and gave her an instant chill. She removed the earpiece.

‘Who’s there?’ she called out, getting off her chair and heading towards the door.

‘Iona, Iona, Iona,’ she heard once again, ‘renounce your Mother Tongue or suffer the consequences.’

‘Who’s there?’ she cried out in anguish grabbing the door handle. She tried to open it but it wouldn’t unlock.

‘Let me out, please. Lionel, where are you?’

‘Iona, Iona, Iona,’ she heard a whispering echo rebounding around the studio, ‘renounce your Mother Tongue or be labelled.’

As she pressed down frantically on the door handle she noticed the reflection of someone in the glass door panel standing in the technical room beyond the studio. She turned around slowly, hoping that her crew were there, hoping the power problem was fixed. But, as she turned around she saw a tall shadowy figure dressed in black whose face was completely obscured.

‘Who are you?’ she asked, transfixed.

As the figure began to move closer towards her, the static began again from within the earpiece.

'Who are you?' she screamed in anguish.

'Penelope,' she could hear Lionel saying faintly. 'Are you okay? The power's back but we've had to move onto the next news item. Penelope,' she could hear him saying over and over.

Penelope looked through the glass that separated her from the technical room relieved to see her crew back in their rightful place and the electricity working. The faceless figure had disappeared leaving Penelope feeling distinctly unnerved. She pondered what had just happened and wondered how the faceless entity had known her Mother Tongue name. She had never divulged it to anyone in Global City.

'You can finish your piece just before the ten o'clock news,' said Lionel.

'It's okay, I said everything I needed to,' said Penelope, not wanting to go back into the studio.

'I'm expecting a back lash from GSW and the GSPC. The first time I don't edit your news report and you decide to take a hammer to Stephen Law's Global vision!'

'Report the truth you told me, remember,' said Penelope.

'Yes, but the truth sometimes comes at a high price,' he said, knowing there would be severe consequences. 'The truth is one thing but being out of business is another.'

As she walked through the newsroom she suddenly felt people were looking at her differently. Nobody said to her great news article or great scoop like they usually would. In fact, as she walked past her colleagues most of them avoided eye contact with her.

‘Hey Louise, how are you?’ she said, hoping for Louise’s usual run down of aches, pains and woes. But she picked up her phone and started a conversation into the mouthpiece.

Penelope sat at her desk and logged onto her computer. She tapped the screen and her biometric print allowed access to her folders. She selected the folder which contained her interview with the Mayor and her report. She looked on screen expecting to see several documents and media files but they were missing. She went into the search facility and typed in Language Town but still the files weren’t there.

Perplexed that she couldn’t find the information she picked up the phone to contact technical support. As Penelope waited for someone to answer, the ring tone suddenly changed to the staccato scraping nose that her earpiece had emitted. The noise penetrated her head which caused her to hang up the phone. Frustrated that she couldn’t find the files and confused by the morning’s events she left her seat to find Lionel.

‘Louise, have I done something to offend you?’ she asked, stopping by her desk.

Louise didn’t answer.

‘Louise, what’s wrong?’ Still silence.

Penelope looked around and was dismayed by the stares and glares from her colleagues.

‘What’s wrong with you all? Is someone going to speak up?’ she shouted. ‘What’s with the silent treatment?’ As Penelope felt an overwhelming frustration build within her soul, she realised that it was her news report that was the problem. She had confessed to being a Mother Tongue native on live Global TV.

‘I’m still the same person. I just speak two languages instead of one. In fact, I speak several languages. Would you like to hear them all?' she shouted, angrily. 'Here we go, which one would you like to hear first? I know, I'll begin with my own Mother Tongue,' she yelled, trying to hold back the tears. She couldn't believe the prejudice that was in the room.

As she was about to monologue in her own language, Lionel entered the room.

'I wouldn't if I were you Penelope. You'll just make the situation worse.'

'What situation?' she asked. He didn't respond.

'I see, silence from you too. You told me to report the truth. You told me I needed to regain my passion. You sent me into that region. You knew what was going on there yet you still sent me.'

'I'm sorry Penelope, I made a mistake. Your report should never have aired.'

'So the files aren't missing, they're destroyed?' 'I'm sorry.'

'You're sorry, you're … ,' Penelope continued in her Mother Tongue.

'Leave the room,' he ordered everyone as Penelope continued verbalising in her Mother Tongue.

As people abandoned their workstations they were unable to leave because the sudden presence of the Language Monitors blocked the exit.

'Stand back,' ordered an audible voice. Penelope looked on, extremely perturbed by the sight of the Language Monitors as they marched in unison towards her.

'What is this?' asked Lionel as he looked at her frightened face.

The Language Monitors did not answer. They seized Penelope and placed her inside the pyramid. They stood motionless awaiting orders.

‘Renounce your Mother Tongue or be labelled,’ the voice boomed into the room.

‘Who is that?’ a few people asked, others said nothing, for fear of being detained. For some, it was fear of being found out. ‘Where’s the voice coming from?’ someone else asked, looking around the room.

‘Renounce your Mother Tongue or accept the consequences,’ roared the voice.

From inside the pyramid, Penelope’s Mother Tongue voice could be heard, ‘I will not renounce my language, culture, identity. Not now, not ever.’

‘Renounce your Mother Tongue or be labelled,’ the voice resounded, one last time.

‘Never,’ replied Penelope, defiantly.

‘Then let the ceremony begin,’ instructed the voice.

The Chief Language Monitor placed the ink stamp and vice on a table in preparation for the labelling ceremony. The people watched in disbelief as Penelope was held against her will. As the labelling ceremony began, the action was livestreamed simultaneously on the TV monitors throughout the building to ensure that all employees saw the humiliation and felt the pain being inflicted upon her. Penelope’s exclamations of anguish in her Mother Tongue could be heard echoing everywhere.

People looked on in horror, relieved that it wasn’t happening to them; gratified that they were pure Global Citizens and the agony Penelope was enduring would never be inflicted on themselves or their loved ones. The illegals in the room were inwardly sweating and praying that their fake IDs were good enough to save them from this tyranny.

As the Language Monitors marched Penelope out of the building to the place that Stephen Law had prepared for the labelled, another labelling ritual aired on the TV monitors at GSW, the GSPC and on live TV in all Global regions. This pre-recorded ritual was in stark contrast to Penelope's.

This latter ceremony did not cause any tribulation to its recipients who were unaware of their starring role. The GS Labelling ceremony that Norman and Linda had unwittingly piloted had Global Citizens flocking to the checkpoint booths in GSW controlled countries. People wanted to ensure they bore the correct label which almost guaranteed their safety and prosperity in Global City, the Motherlands and those countries which had sworn allegiance to Stephen Law. However, Norman and Linda had no idea that they were now the faces of this ceremony, the footage of which Stephen Law had personally edited and was now airing to all GSW endorsed regions.

As Penelope was delivered to the Language Monitor truck which would transport her directly to be with the other language traitors Rod was puzzled why Stephen had not made his holographic appearance as he had in Area Blue. As Rod watched the proceedings on his mini pc, he was also perturbed because he did not recognise the voice that everyone had heard barking instructions. Whose voice it was he did not know but it was most definitely NOT that of Stephen Law.

42

Penelope's confession and her willingness to stand with other language traitors had rocked Stephen to the core. As he watched Penelope's footage he thought back to Global Standard launch day when he had been caught off-guard by Norman's photographs of his hometown and of Grigor. He was dismayed that he had yet again been surprised and his hometown had been thrust upon him, unwittingly. However, this time was much worse because the place and people were not in stills format; but were moving about in real life. Stephen had muted Penelope's footage so he didn't have to endure hearing his language.

He zoomed in on Grigor's face; a face he had once loved; a face he had once trusted and from whom he had never wanted to be parted. He paused the clip and observed Grigor's smiling, happy demeanour. Suddenly Stephen felt endeared by his teenage friend and momentarily questioned the purpose of his GS vision.

'Stephen, Stephen, Stephen,' said the familiar voice. 'Do not be taken in by sentiment. Feelings are fleeting. Emotion is short lived. What do you want to be remembered for? Sentiment or status?'

The Invisible Stranger's harsh words brought Stephen back to his senses.

'Press play,' instructed the Invisible Stranger. 'I've seen enough,' said Stephen.

'Press play,' he demanded. 'There's something else you need to see.'

Stephen pressed play and the clip resumed. Stephen watched Penelope and Grigor laughing and chatting, but then the camera zoomed out and focused on a different shot, a woman who was walking towards them.

The camera returned to Penelope who seemed to be making an introduction. Then the woman came into the camera's view and shook hands with Penelope. The Invisible Stranger unmuted the recording.

'It's a pleasure to meet you, Mrs. Mayor,' broadcast Penelope, greeting Aphia. Stephen watched in silence, understanding each and every word. The Invisible Stranger muted the recording once more.

Stephen had an overwhelming pain in his chest as he realised that Mrs. Mayor was Joan, his Joan, his constant who had left him and never returned. Stephen pressed pause and Joan's familiar face was freeze-framed on the screen. His heart ached like the day he had lost Apollos.

Despair engulfed him as he questioned why Joan would have converted from a Global to a Mother Tongue citizen. He couldn't process how she had ended up in his home town and was married to Grigor. Was this even real? Was this a deception by the Invisible Stranger?

'How can she speak another language so well after such a short time?' he wondered, perplexed.

'Stephen, Stephen, Stephen, did I not just say that sentiment won't get you anywhere. It's time to return to your homeland and make Area Orange an epicentre for Global Standard. It's time to herald a return to Babel. It's time to show the world that you are the law! It's time for the language traitors to be punished.'

'Who are you?' the brooding presence asked determinedly but Stephen could only focus on Joan and her conversion to Mother Tongue and marriage to of all people, Grigor.

'Who are you?' the brooding presence asked repeatedly inciting outrage in Stephen's whole being.

'I am Stephen Law.'

'Who are you?'

‘I am the law, I am the law, I AM the law,’ Stephen repeated over and over until every ounce of sentiment had drained from his inner core.

43

Stephen looked through the one-way glass to see his new constant, Claudia, sat at her workstation. He watched her as she worked, unable to get the image of Joan's face out of his head. He remembered nostalgically how Joan had the same routine each night she'd left work. She would wait dutifully until he dismissed her for the day. Then she would respond, "Thank you, Sir, have a nice evening." Then, in the same methodical manner she would walk effortlessly to the lift, with her coat draped over her left arm and handbag dangled on her right wrist. He recalled how he thought that her name, Joan, did not suit her. It seemed out of place for someone of her generation.

'Joan,' he said out loud over and over. The more he said her name the more incensed he became. 'Joan, Joan, Joan,' he said in the same patronising tone that he'd used with Rod, relieved that his yearning for her to return to Global City and resume her role, had been short lived.

'Joan and Grigor,' he thought, callously. 'My teenage friend and the former secretary to the leader of the free Global world; opposites most certainly do attract. This would explain why you never returned.' Stephen pondered how Joan, after leaving Global City had ended up, in all places, in his hometown, married to his nemesis.

'Joan, Joan, Joan,' he kept saying aloud and suddenly he remembered the old CCTV footage.

'How did I forget that?' he puzzled, as he accessed the CCTV archives on his computer. Stephen pressed play on the stored recording.

"I have completed the task as you requested," he heard Phoebe say to Joan.

“Thank you, you may leave. Goodnight,” said Joan.

“Thank you. Have a nice evening, Miss Marsh,” said Phoebe.

As he had done the first time, he watched the CCTV, replaying the footage. He slowed Joan’s words, ensuring that he hadn’t missed anything.

‘There,’ he thought, ‘right there, that’s what I detected before but I didn’t realise its significance.’ He re-ran the dialogue several times to confirm his suspicions.

“Thank you. Have a nice evening,” he played again and again; first Joan, then Phoebe. Using the advanced playback facility, he isolated Joan’s voice saying, “Thank you. Have a nice evening.” He did the same with Phoebe’s. Then, he replayed the voices simultaneously and to his disbelief both had identical accents.

As he listened obsessively, it became obvious that Joan and Phoebe had the same intonation. It was then he realised of whom Joan’s voice had reminded him – it was Grigor, his parents, Apollos and Jakov – it was everyone that he had ever known from his hometown – himself included.

‘Joan is a Mother Tongue Citizen,’ he boomed audibly. ‘Joan is from my own country. How did I not know?’ he cried out in anger.

‘Tell Phoebe Burnham to attend my office immediately,’ he ordered Claudia.

‘Sorry, Mr. Law? You want Miss Burnham to physically attend your office?’

‘Yes, right away.’

‘Very well,’ she replied, alarmed that he wanted an employee to share his office space. Nobody, except Rod Jones and the Head Language Monitor, ever went into his office. ‘It must be bad,’ thought Claudia, dialling Phoebe’s extension number.

Phoebe stood with her head cast down in front of Mr. Law's desk waiting for him to speak. Her insides shook with the uncertainty of his summons. Her eyes scanned the floor and stopped at the sight of his briefcase. She had heard many stories about the mysterious bag and how it was seemingly attached to him, twenty-four hours a day. There were many tales about what was in the bag. Phoebe looked intently at the bag but it was completely sealed.

Stephen looked up, 'Miss Burnham, tell me about your Mother Tongue and hometown,' he began.

She looked up at his face and couldn't help staring into his eyes which were blood shot.

'What would you like to know specifically, Sir?' she asked, trying to hide her fear and confused by his question. She had already admitted her illegal status and renounced her Mother Tongue. He knew all there was to know about her which had ensured her amnesty in Global City. There had been no repercussions regarding her previous illegal status.

'Can you pinpoint your homeland on the GSW world map?' he asked, calmly. Phoebe walked towards the interactive wall. She was taken aback by how many countries were coloured black.

'This is my homeland, Sir,' she said, pointing to Area Orange.

'And tell me, Miss Burnham, as far as you are aware, where on the GSW map does Joan Marsh originate?'

'Miss Marsh?' she queried, alarmed by his question.

'Yes, the ex-secretary to the leader of the free Global world. Where does she come from? Do you know?'

Phoebe looked at Stephen sheepishly wondering if he knew the truth about Joan. She didn't know what to do. If she pointed to Motherland what would he do to her and her sister? If she pointed to Area Orange, which would indicate that she had known Joan's secret all along, what would be the repercussions?

'It's not a trick question Miss Burnham. Indicate on the map. I'll give you a few moments,' he said.

Phoebe's eyes reluctantly scanned Area Orange and the Motherland.

'Time's up,' he said, calmly. 'So, Miss Burnham, from where does Miss Marsh come? Is she a native Global speaker from Motherland or, like you, does she originate from a Mother Tongue country and purposely deceived the leader of the free Global world? Which is it?'

Phoebe looked in trepidation at his eyes which were blood shot and watering. His face, which she found handsome, looked in pain, as if he wanted to know the truth but couldn't bear the answer.

Phoebe lifted her right arm slowly and extended her index finger which shook unsteadily. Her finger hovered in mid-air, preparing to select a region. She looked at the menacing black hue of Motherland and then to the refreshing orange label of her own country. She felt tears well in the back of her eyes as her index finger poised.

She sensed there were consequences attached to each label. Phoebe closed her eyes as she selected the orange of her own country. She opened them moments later to see Stephen Law sitting at his desk.

'That will be all,' he said, calmly. 'You will not divulge this information to anyone.'

'Yes Sir, of course. Thank you,' she said, relief flowing through her body.

'You may leave,' ordered Stephen.

Stephen looked intently at the sweaty fingerprint left by Phoebe when she had selected Area Orange.

***

‘It’s time to advance in the name of Global. It’s time to develop the land I‘ve purchased in Area Orange. It’s time to herald a return to Babel; it’s time to show the world that I AM the law! It’s time for the language traitors to be punished. It’s time … ,’ he told himself, fanatically, while the Invisible Stranger smiled in glee.

44

'What do you mean I am leaving Global City?' asked Phoebe.

'You are being reassigned,' confirmed Rod.

'To where?' asked Phoebe confused.

'You'll know when you get there.'

'Who else is being reassigned? Are my sister and friends?'

You don't need to know. Be prepared to leave at short notice. Until then, carry on as usual,' instructed Rod, not divulging she would be joining him in Area Orange.

45

As Mother Tongue citizens in Area Orange awoke, they were confused by the transmission of a strange, red glow that infiltrated their homes. Equally, Mother Tongue citizens living in the mountain village were curious about the structure that housed the bright neon red sign, shining in the distance. One citizen, in particular, was extremely concerned about the message Phoebe's grandmother placed her binoculars on the kitchen table and deliberated how she could make her way into town. Her legs wouldn't carry her and she didn't have another mode of transport. But she knew she had to get there somehow.

Pondering what this intrusive reflection could be, Mother Tongue citizens hurriedly followed the light and flocked to the land that once housed the protected species; the land that the Mayor had sold without public knowledge or consent of the townsfolk. This land now lodged a purpose built mantra that did not belong there.

As the tourists who were paying for a language town experience awoke; they too couldn't believe their eyes. They were dumbfounded as they looked at the Global Standard message that dominated the skyline unable to connect the town's mantra with the Global motto. Some understood its message; some didn't. For those who did, they wondered why there was such a prominent Global structure impinging on their "no Global" holiday.

Grigor woke abruptly startled by a neon red intrusive hue that was flooding his bedroom. He blinked a few times thinking that his eyes were the problem but the same red tinge remained. Opening his curtains reinforced that his eyes were fine, but the view wasn't. He stood aghast looking at the intrusive sign that had been constructed on the land he'd sold to a stranger.

'What's that strange light?' asked Aphia, still dozing. Suddenly, a strange sense of waking in Global City thwacked her senses. Grigor didn't answer; he hurriedly got dressed and rushed outside.

As Grigor looked at the screen in disbelief, unable to understand the message as it wasn't in Mother Tongue, another beam of light caused everyone to cover their eyes. The first light was dim in comparison to this.

The screen displayed the "One Language, One Version, One Vision" in audacious neon red.

Global Citizen's raised voices and rushing feet marched towards Grigor. Hundreds of voices were questioning him, pointing their fingers, encircling him like a captured animal.

'What does it mean?' Mother Tongue citizens were demanding.

'How is it here? When did it arrive...?' multiple questions filled the air.

Of course, some tourists and closet Global speakers could understand the sign but they didn't want to speak in Global while in the Language Town.

'What is it?' Mother Tongue citizens demanded again, their voices becoming louder and louder. 'What does it mean?'

A tourist turned to Grigor and said in broken Mother Tongue, 'May I translate for you? It's written in Global Standard.'

Grigor was mystified. There was that phrase again, Global Standard! How had any version of Global entered his NO GLOBAL town?

By now Aphia was standing by his side and, unknown to Grigor, she knew full well what the sign said. Dread filled her whole body as she sensed Stephen Law's presence.

'How has he found me?' she questioned, dismayed that her lies were encircling her.

Aphia's eyes were instantly drawn to the woods and she saw the same eerie figure moving slowly yet confidently towards her as on that day she and Grigor had trekked up the mountain. As the outline moved closer, Aphia could see that the dark clothing was actually a navy suit. A champagne-coloured tie adorned his chest. In his breast pocket nestled a navy and cream polka dot handkerchief. His white faceless expression became familiar to her; except today, the faceless figure had greying hair. He motioned her to come. She was transfixed and unable to move or speak as she realised the figure was Stephen Law and that he was here, in her hometown, beckoning her. She wasn't imagining his presence.

'Who is that?' asked Grigor, perplexed.

Grigor looked at Aphia whose complexion was ashen, just like the other times when she'd felt unwell.

'Do you know him?' demanded Grigor. Aphia was flummoxed.

'Do I lie one more time or do I tell Grigor the truth?' she deliberated, 'before Stephen does.'

'Why is he summoning you? Who is he?' 'Oh Grigor, please forgive me.'

'Forgive you for what?'

'I'm so sorry,' she said, as she walked towards Stephen.

'Aphia, where are you going? Who is that man?' he yelled after her.

As Grigor watched Aphia walk away, he could hear the noise of fresh marching feet in the distance. But this time it sounded planned, precision-like, in sync.

'What is this?' he questioned, deeply perturbed at the sight of the Language Monitors invading his homeland, bearing a flag that bore the same Global Standard message that beamed from the structure. 'Who would have the audacity to bring Global so boldly into my town?' he demanded, feeling despair that he hadn't fulfilled his promise to Jakov and Apollos.

Aphia looked over her shoulder to Grigor and then to Stephen Law in the near distance. She glanced back and fore, seeing the parallel world they both inhabited; both desperate to keep a language out; but with different motives.

Oblivious to the intensity of the situation, the tourist continued. The message says, "This land will be the proud host of the first Global Standard Language School and will offer free education to all Mother Tongue Citizens." Sheepishly, she continued, "One Language, One Version, One Vision."

'What have I done? What have I done?' muttered Grigor, falling to his knees. 'I have let Global in; how could this be? How could I have I betrayed Apollos and Jakov's memory and my own family? What have I done?' he kept repeating over and over.

Hearing Grigor's cries of anguish, Aphia ran back to him.

'Please help him up,' she pleaded, as she witnessed this pitiful version of her husband, 'please … ,' she continued as Mother Tongue citizens turned their backs on Grigor, shunning this version of their Mayor. They didn't care how Grigor was feeling and one by one they followed the Language Monitors as they marched towards the structure.

'We will help him,' said two tourists in Global, as Aphia watched every Mother Tongue citizen walk away. Mother Tongue citizens were in disbelief that Grigor had sold out to Global after all. That he had deceived them and selling the protected land was not about protecting their land and heritage it was all about money; Global money. Of course, the only person who knew the whole truth could not speak up, not now at least.

'Why here?' Aphia pondered, 'why this minute part of the world?' wondering if this Global conquest was because of The Language Town and their opposition to Global or had Stephen Law found her location? Was this retribution for deserting him? She had no idea that Stephen Law's connection to the town was rooted much deeper.

As Grigor was helped to his feet, Aphia continued to look yonder. She was in disbelief at this surreal scene in her home town with the neon red basking in glory. The Language Monitors had formed a barrier and Mother Tongue citizens were penned in waiting for an explanation from someone – they didn't care from whom, they just wanted an explanation.

Citizens were restless and Aphia noticed that groups had quickly formed within the crowd. One group was listening intently to a man perched on an old crate, his face and neck straining from talking loudly. His hand gestures were elaborate and the more support he gained from his onlookers the bolder he became. Whatever he was saying drew attention from other groups of people who soon joined in. She turned to ask Grigor how he was going to explain the situation but he had slipped away without her noticing. She knew that the only place he'd be was in his office.

'Grigor, you must address your citizens. You cannot hide in here. You have made a mistake … .'

She painfully considered if this was the time to confess her involvement with Global. To confess that she knew what the sign read before the tourist's interpretation. She knew that time was against her and Stephen

Law's presence amongst the people was imminent.

'He warned me years ago, not to touch it. He told me it was a box of evil and it can make you do things you don't want to,' he babbled, looking up at Aphia with tears in his eyes.

'Who warned you? What box of evil?' Aphia asked confused.

Remember we talked about my childhood friend Nastan Popov and how no one has ever heard from or seen him since he left town. How, I've been expecting him, that I've anticipated his visit but so far no sign of him – the language traitor.'

'Yes, I remember, of course I do because you seemed so distressed by the whole thing,' said Aphia, wondering if Grigor was also making the connection.

The Global papers I sent him were meant to drive him insane. They were meant to make him as unhappy as I was when he left. They were meant to drive him into obscurity. He should have spent his adult life in despair and feeling ashamed that his own father tried to eliminate our language.

'His father, what was his involvement in all this?'

'His father sparked it all. His father was the original language traitor. He wanted to trade Mother Tongue for Global. He was the Language Ambassador for Global within our country. All those years ago, his father began his own legacy that ended abruptly. Tragedy struck because of Global.'

'What happened?'

'Nastan's father, Stephen, was due to make a speech that would have ushered in a new Global wave.'

'Nastan's father's name was Stephen?'

'Yes, ironic how it actually sounds more like a Global name than a Mother Tongue one. Maybe that was Apollos' first mistake concerning his son. One day, I was at home when a package arrived for Nastan. His grandfather had just died and he was living with my family. The package was from the bank. I pretended to the courier that I was Nastan and took receipt of the delivery. A briefcase, a black briefcase, that actually looked more like a small suitcase because of the wheels.'

Aphia's stomach churned as Grigor described the infamous briefcase that never left Stephen possession.

I unzipped it and there they were, his father's original papers, the blueprint for Global replacing Mother Tongue. Apollos had kept them deposited at the bank for all those years and his death had freed them. Except, I burned the Mother Tongue version and left only the Global. I hid the papers, here, in Jakov's den but Jakov found them. Instead of reprimanding me for my actions, we made a pact to keep Global out, no matter what; no matter what the cost. Global had to stay away. Then, in my anger, I ensured the Global papers travelled with Nastan to that treacherous International School. I wanted him to spend his entire life trying to translate them in full knowledge that his father was not a hero but a language traitor who would have sold his soul to the devil.

'The Global papers; the papers that I sent to Nastan Popov all those years ago out of spite and anger; I wanted his obsession with Global to become his downfall. But it seems that after all these years MY obsession with Global has become MY downfall.

'After Apollos' death, when Nastan left town for the International School, I stayed and swore an allegiance to never, ever let Global into our country, our town or our lives. Jakov fought with his dying breath to protect our language, culture and heritage and now, my failure to succeed, my failure to protect this beloved land has let Global in. How has this happened? How …?'

Aphia looked at this unrecognisable version of Grigor, sat at his desk, looking out of the window at the neon red sign that sealed his failure.

As Grigor continued with his assassination of his own character, she too looked at the sign that was a painful reminder of her life in Global City and how she needed to tell Grigor the truth about Stephen Law. She needed to tell him everything before Stephen did.

Grigor continued, 'But of course, we - me and Jakov, we needed to know what the papers said but they were in Global and nobody in town spoke Global; at least nobody who would admit it publicly. Then, Jakov confessed that he could speak it.'

'Jakov, the Mayor, spoke Global!' interrupted Aphia. Yes, but not out of choice but necessity because he had been forced to learn it as a child. He told me that Global left a bad taste in his mouth, but his ability to translate the papers ensured that Global stayed out of our country. Doctor Mitrov ensured that Jakov's ability to speak Global remained a secret. Can you imagine how the people would have reacted! His sedation was a necessary act.'

'Sedation! What are you saying Grigor?'

'Just before he died, Jakov began speaking Global in what could only be described as fits of consciousness. We couldn't allow him to speak Global publicly and of course the whole town wanted to pay their respects before he passed, so Doctor Mitrov made sure Jakov was asleep whenever someone came to visit.'

Aphia couldn't believe that a doctor had acted in this way; a doctor who was still practising medicine, despite the fact that he should have retired years ago because of his age!

Grigor got out of his chair and walked into the den. Aphia stared intently out of the window that had a clear view of the land in disbelief that her outlook had changed overnight; in astonishment that her new life was now an abridged version of that in Global City.

Aphia heard an odd squeaking noise coming from the den.

'Grigor, what are you doing?' she asked, alarmed, as she saw him sat on Jakov's ancient office chair with his back to her. He had refused to throw the relic out. The squeaking noise was being made by Grigor's rocking motion which was piercing the room.

'Grigor, you have to address your citizens, this is no time to act like … I don't even know what you're acting like,' she said to him abruptly.

Grigor spun the chair slowly and the high-pitched squeak caused Aphia to cover her ears. Grigor was clutching the documents that Jakov had locked away in the cupboard all those years ago; the documents that Jakov had made Grigor promise no one would ever see.

'What are those?' asked Aphia, curiously.

'You can't see them?' responded Grigor, almost childlike.

'Give them to me,' she said, feeling peeved that hiding paperwork from her had got them into this situation to start with.

'No, you can't see them. I am going to burn them. I made a promise to Jakov.'

'Jakov is gone, Grigor, and we are here in this state, so you need to tell me the whole truth before whoever it is that has purchased the land and is promising prosperity to your citizens, addresses them. If you do not salvage this situation you will be ousted as Mayor, because the person that is about to address this town will not be slinking away like you. The person who erected that sign will … .'

'Here,' said G rigor, standing up and handing over the files. 'This is everything you need to know.'

Grigor placed everything into Aphia's hands and left the den. He sat in the visitor's chair in his office. He didn't feel worthy to sit on the Mayor's chair at the Mayor's desk.

Unbeknownst to Grigor, Aphia was capable of reading and understanding the Global papers he had thrust at her.

'Grigor, time is against us. What do you expect me to do with these documents? You would be better off reading the land purchase agreement to see how we can get ourselves out of this mess. Whatever you signed has allowed Global in and this is what you need to take care of. What are you going to tell the townsfolk?'

Grigor stood up and looked out of the office window. 'I truthfully don't know,' he said, 'but it's too late now anyway.'

'What do you mean?'

'He's here … Nastan Popov is here, just as Jakov feared all those years ago. Nastan Popov has let Global in.'

Aphia joined Grigor at the window and watched as Stephen Law and Rod Jones made their way over to the crowd.

46

'Mother Tongue citizens,' Stephen began in Global; his words being simultaneously translated into Mother Tongue and displayed on the digital screen. Stephen wore noise cancelling ear phones so he didn't have to tolerate his Mother Tongue.

As he spoke his voice got louder to ensure that his words weren't diminished by the marching of the Language Monitors. Strangely, Mother Tongue citizens didn't seem threatened by their presence but instead were transfixed by Stephen Law and what he had to offer. Each citizen was handed a Translate Technology Device.

Stephen explained to the crowd that he had bought the land at the behest of the Mayor because their town was in financial trouble and this was the only way to secure jobs, houses and education. He further clarified that he could provide each person with a prosperous future in the name of Global Standard and all they needed to do was learn the language by using their new devices which would expedite their Global Standard knowledge.

As he continued to offer Mother Tongue citizens hope and prosperity, he played a short film of his version of the future. The townsfolk looked at each other, nodding and smiling. Their Mayor had offered them prosperity and security but he hadn't delivered on his promises. The Language Town had nearly ruined them financially. This new version of their way of life seemed much more enticing and believable. Grigor looked on in disbelief at his citizens who seemed entranced by whatever lies Nastan was telling them.

'I will not allow Nastan Popov to undo years and years of hard work and history,' yelled Grigor, making his way towards his office door. But, sadly, his determination to act had come too late.

'What's that noise?' asked Aphia, as the Language Monitors entered the town hall. They stood guard at the main entrance while other Language Monitors deployed in groups of three pursuing Mother Tongue citizens.

'Grigor, don't open the door,' said Aphia, sensing she needed to make a quick confession. 'There's something I need to tell you; I've been meaning to tell you since the day we met but there never seemed to be the right moment.'

As Aphia's GSW colleagues entered the Mayor's office and surrounded her until she was in the centre of the pyramid, she knew it was too late to tell Grigor the truth.

'Quick step,' the head of the pyramid commanded, as the other two grabbed her arms and marched her away from Grigor.

'It's me, Joan,' she cried out in Global to the Language Monitors. 'Don't you recognise me?'

As she was marched away, Grigor watched in shock as Aphia spoke Global; he'd heard the language enough over the years to recognise it.

'Aphia,' he called after her in Mother Tongue.

'I'm sorry, I can explain,' she cried out to him, 'I can explain. Please forgive me. They won't hurt me, don't worry. They know me. Don't worry.'

Grigor, not caring what Aphia had done, but just wanting to rescue her from this surreal situation was himself surrounded by Language Monitors. They had been instructed by Stephen Law to put him onto a Language Monitor truck and ensure that Mother Tongue citizens did not see him being captured. As far as Stephen was concerned he wanted Mother Tongue citizens to believe that Grigor had deserted them, his wife, their town and way of life.

As Grigor was herded away in the LM truck, he watched, through the open wooden slats as Aphia made her way towards Nastan Popov. The Language Monitors had loosened their grip of her and this gave him some solace.

'Aphia,' he cried out in anguish but she did not hear.

'Aphia,' he cried out, his voice diminishing in the realisation that his citizens would believe that he had abandoned them and worst still, he had deserted Aphia too.

As Aphia locked eyes with Stephen Law, Aphia sensed an air of familiarity. As they got closer Stephen held out his hands. To Aphia's surprise Stephen was holding her mini pc and Global Citizen identity card.

'Welcome back, Miss Marsh,' said Stephen soberly as he placed the items in her hands.

Mother Tongue citizens watched as Aphia stood face to face with Stephen Law, believing that she was picking up the pieces of Grigor's desertion; not that she was being reinstated to her rightful place as secretary to the leader of the free Global world. Equally, they had no inclination that Stephen Law was of Mother Tongue heritage, as are they … .

THE RISE OF GLOBAL: BABEL

By Donna Lent

Due to be published in 2024 is the final book in *THE RISE OF GLOBAL* trilogy.

Printed in Great Britain
by Amazon

58860988R00131